Memories Can't
Be Replaced

Memories Can't
Be Replaced

Brittney C. Nobles

Library of Congress Control Number:		2020911342
ISBN:	Hardcover	978-1-9845-8479-3
	Softcover	978-1-9845-8478-6
	eBook	978-1-9845-8477-9

Print information available on the last page.

Rev. date: 06/18/2020

To order additional copies of this book, contact:
Xlibris
1-888-795-4274
www.Xlibris.com
Orders@Xlibris.com
809126

PROLOGUE

Vince Martin looked over at his beautiful wife, Chasity, and smiled as they headed back to their home in Rincon, Georgia. The two went grocery shopping for their three children before picking up their youngest, LaKennon, from basketball practice. Their twin daughters, LaSiah and LaShae, were at home on punishment for skipping school the day before. Chasity hated punishing her children, but it was necessary for the girls to learn their lesson.

Vince and Chasity have been married for twenty-seven years. They have a total of four children. Their eldest lives in New Bern, North Carolina. She moved out and away when she was eighteen. New Bern is where the Martin family is originally from.

LaKennon had his headphones on when he got into the SUV. He didn't even muster a simple hello to his parents. He threw his gym bag on the backseat before making himself comfortable. The couple looked at each other, not surprised by his actions. Lately, the Martin household has been equivalent to a boot camp. Vince is an ex-marine and his idea of getting his children to mind is with military drills. They hated it, but Vince took pleasure in their suffering.

The fifteen-minute ride from the high school to their home was silent. Vince was speeding as usual. Chasity didn't like the way her husband drove, nor did she like driving. As the SUV traveled down the road at an excessive speed, Vince pressed the brake to slow down a bit, but the brake pedal went straight to the floor. He tried several times more, with no success. Chasity was becoming afraid, her husband drove fast, but not that fast. Even LaKennon started to become worried. He took his headphones off to ask his dad what was going on. Vince didn't want to upset his son or wife, so he lied, playing it off as if he meant to go that fast. He was becoming scared. He had no control over the vehicle, he was hopeless. He prayed as hard as he could to himself. He prayed for safety for his family. As he tried to press the brakes again Chasity noticed his actions. She asked her husband the same question her son previously asked. No answer. He looked at his wife with so much endearment, he whispered I love you. Then the 2015 Chevrolet Tahoe flipped a total of nine times before crashing into a tree.

CHAPTER 1

"LaSiah, wake up," my twin sister, LaShae said to me this good morning. I haven't even been up for three seconds and she's already getting on my damn nerves. Today was moving day, and to say I'm not ready would be an understatement. 1 year and 6 months ago, our parents were fatally killed in a car accident. Although the crash claimed the lives of our parents, our brother's life was spared. LaKennon has been in critical condition since that day. He is showing progress for improvement, but the doctor still thinks a medically induced coma is best to heal his body inside and out. LaShae, LaKendra, and I had to plan our parents' funeral on our own. It was the hardest day of my life. My sister and I are moving to New Bern with LaKendra and her boyfriend, Peanut. I'm not really happy about the move because my whole entire life lies in Effingham County. I literally cried the entire night.

The reason we have to move is that we can't afford the mortgage by ourselves anymore, although we got money from our parents' social security it's not enough for us to continue to live in our home. The lawyer advised us to move in with our older sister so that we can save the money for when we need it the most. Our parents had money saved up and plus life insurance. To stay in Georgia will be like continuing to throw our money down a rat hole. Moving to North Carolina we will continue to get money monthly and a portion will go into the savings account our parents started for us when we were born.

I'm going to miss my best friend, Aaron so much. Man, fuck! To make matters worse we are leaving LaKennon here all by himself, but I have made a promise to myself to come to see him every chance I get. My sisters and I decided to keep him in the care of the doctors who know him well rather than uprooting him to a new hospital with new doctors. Hopefully, he will recover soon then he will come to live in North Carolina too.

I showered then loaded the rest of my things into my black 2016 Honda Accord. We shipped most of our belongings months ago. What we didn't want, we sold. LaShae's identical, but white car was already loaded and ready for takeoff. Maybe this six-hour drive will bring my spirits up about moving. Even though we are technically *from* New Bern, I still don't want to move there. Too many nosey ass family members reside there. Where there is family, there is also a hand sticking out from one of them, as if getting a job to make their own money is illegal.

We pulled off, and I couldn't stand to turn around to look at our beautiful home for the last time. I wish life were different, but things happen for a reason. LaShae and I don't talk about the accident or our parents that much. We weren't on the best of terms with them during the time of their deaths. LaKennon probably snitched on us, younger brother problems. LaShae and I skipped class to get our nails done. I mean we are sophomores in college, we should be allowed at least one free day. My parents were too strict, no wonder I'm still a virgin. LaShae not so much. I'm not going to comment on her sex experiences, because it's none of my business. I worry about my pussy and mine only. I want my first time to be special with someone special. I don't want to give my virginity away without proper consideration. Aaron and LaShae always teased me for holding out so long, but I rather. I've seen them both give their bodies to someone who won't even remember their names the next week. But all that is in the past now. Our parents are in the past. Georgia is in the past. North Carolina is now our future.

CHAPTER 2

I was exhausted by the time we reached New Bern. Kendra greeted us from her front porch. Her two-story house was attained from our paternal grandmother, she moved into a one-bedroom apartment and gave the house to Kendra to occupy. As soon as we got out the car Kendra rushed up to us and gave us a huge hug. She's the lovey-dovey type, I don't know where she got that from because our parents didn't embrace us or pet us up. Tough love, or no love. Our mother used to try to show some type of affection, but it was only awkward. Peanut was right behind her to greet us. He was clearly tipsy, but that was Peanut. We met him a couple of summers back before they started dating. Always loud, and always tipsy. He reeked of beer, almost like it was coming from his pores. Peanut helped put our suitcases in our bedrooms upstairs. My bedroom is alright, it's gonna get better when I add my touches to it. I rested on my new bed, I needed to rest my body after that drive.

My sisters and I are extremely close; we tell each other everything. One can't take a shit without the other one knowing. I am excited to see our relationship grow even more now that we will all be under the same roof.

After resting for a couple of minutes, I pulled out my cell phone to call Aaron.

"What's up girl? You there yet?" He asked.

"Yes, I'm here," I said exhaustingly. "I'm just a little tired. I miss you already." I admitted.

"I miss you too, when are you gonna come back?"

"I'm not sure, we have to get everything straight here first. Since

I transferred to this community college, the new semester starts Monday and I have to mentally prepare myself." We talked until I fell asleep on him. I love Aaron and I'm going to miss him so much. I don't know what I'm gonna do without him, he's the greatest best-friend a girl can ask for. A slight knock fell upon my bedroom door. It was Shae.

I sat up. She rolled her eyes as soon as she entered my room and I already knew what was on her mind. She has never cared for Peanut and she doesn't have a problem expressing it. My twin is so damn evil, but I love it. She's the yin to my yang. Shae and I are identical twins. Except she's a lighter complexion than me. We aren't the skinniest of girls in the world, nor are we heavy set. We are plump in all the right places. Where she lacks, I pick up. My boobs are bigger than hers, but her butt is bigger than mine, slightly. We have shoulder-length *relaxed* hair, hers is a light brown and mine is jet black. I stress relaxed because every bitch in this generation thinks it's cute to go natural. I wish I could do a public service announcement saying, Natural is not for every bitch. Our eyes are grayish. My mole on my chin sets us more apart. "Shae, you need to relax. Did you unpack?"

"Hell No, but I came in here for something," she paused for a second, jogging her memory. "Oh! Kendra said she's throwing us a welcome party tonight."

"What?!" I questioned confused. Can we get settled first, and Kendra is not a party person so why would she throw us a party? I'm not complaining, I can't wait to meet new people. I'm ready to see my childhood friend, Yazzy. I haven't seen her in years, but we talk every month. I used to come to New Bern almost every summer just to get away from my parent's rule. Yazzy and I hung out every day, all day. "What time is this party supposed to start?"

"I believe at seven. Let me borrow your yellow halter top with the ruffles around the cleavage area."

"No, that's one of my favorite shirts," I rolled my eyes at her because she knows that. Simple ass, what's wrong with her own shit? I thought to myself.

"Please, please, please," she begged. "I got to look good." She strutted across the room as if she was a model. I tried to hold my laughter in. This girl is so full of herself, it's ridiculous.

"Look good in your own shit." I went to my packed suitcases to find me something to wear. Talking about she gotta look good, shit my ass gotta look good. I put her out of my room so I could concentrate on myself. I managed to find the yellow top, but I hid it in a drawer with some other clothes. I did, however, decide to wear my black blazer with a silk tank top and some blue jeans. I threw on some red wedges to complete the look, by the time I flat ironed my hair it was 6:30 p.m. and I was ready to go. I headed downstairs with my new live-in family. "I'm ready to go," I announced. Kendra, Peanut, and Shae looked at me like I was crazy.

"Ready to go where?" Kendra asked looking me up and down.

"To this party."

They all shared a laugh. Their laughter irritated me. "The party is right here girl. We ain't going no damn where. Peanut is about to move the couches so we can get lit. Kendra and I made a liquor store run before the official party started. I had to have some rum. Kendra got all types of liquor, I don't know how many people she invited, but from the looks of the many bottles she had, it seemed like the whole entire city. No way I would have spent that much at the liquor store, the party would have been B.Y.O.L, bring your own liquor. I can't supply the whole entire neighborhood. But hey, better her than me. Guests started to show a quarter after eight. Shae and I were already pre-gaming before the crowd arrived. I downed my bottle of rum within minutes. I cannot party sober, but I can't hold my liquor either. I started to feel a little queasy, so I excused myself so I could lay down for a bit. I couldn't get comfortable with all the loud music blaring in the house. I tossed and turned for about fifteen minutes, and my stomach was not feeling any better.

I closed my eyes and entered my own serenity. My mind drifted back to my parents. I miss them. They never taught us how to live without them. If they were still here, I would hug them every day, and I'd promise to follow all their rules, but most importantly I would tell them how much they mean to me. I have to succeed in life…for them.

My thoughts were interrupted when my bedroom door flung open and the light turned on. The light hurt my eyes, I buried them in my pillow.

"My bad, yo. I was looking for the bathroom," the intruder said.

Without lifting my head from the pillow, I pointed, "It's the next door," I muffled. The intruder apologized again. Then it hit me before the intruder could close the door I jumped up, pushed past him to the bathroom. I threw up all over the toilet seat. I felt his eyes on me and I immediately became embarrassed. He leaned on the door frame peering at me. My vision was blurred, and I couldn't make out his face. I should've used my bedroom's bathroom, but I didn't want to mess it up or smell puke in my room.

"Damn girl, you iight?" He asked. Being so embarrassed all I could do was nod my head. This has got to be the worst experience I have had with alcohol. I'm never drinking this much at a party again. I hugged the toilet as if it was my best friend. I wiped my mouth as I tried to stand, I stumbled, and he had to grab my arm so I didn't fall. He then sat me on the side of the tub like I was a baby, "You're fucked up, yo," he laughed. I giggled a little to hide my shame. He took a nearby decorative cloth to wipe the puke from my chin. I don't know this man from Adam or Eve and here he is cleaning up after me like he's known me his entire life. That spoke volumes to me. I don't think I could've done that for anybody, especially someone I don't even know. He helped me back to my room, I laid back on my bed in a fetal position. "You good?" He asked. I nodded again. He left. The party was still going on, I could hear the deejay calling all the ladies to the 'dance floor' aka the middle of the living room. Now that my stomach was feeling better, I got myself together, changed my clothes and brushed my teeth. I did not want anyone to know I just puked my brains out, besides the mystery man. I returned to the party like I never left. It was a full-on twerk session when I made it to the bottom step. I wasn't completely sober, but I wasn't pissy drunk anymore either. I hoped to find the guy that helped me earlier to thank him for his hospitality. I searched the room, but I didn't see anyone who had on the same colors as him. I jumped on the dance floor to enjoy a dance or two, I noticed Shae in the corner all over some guy, but

I minded my own business and kept on dancing to the jams. The deejay knows how to keep the party jumping. One of the guys I danced with earlier came behind me. We dance through two or three more songs. I was tired as hell. Twerking does take a lot out of you. The fourth song started, and I was still getting my twerk on with this dude when another guy asked to cut in. I didn't even turn around to look at him, dance is a dance. I have no problem dancing with guys, but most of them think just because I danced on him for a couple of songs means I want him. But I don't, I just like to enjoy myself. The new guy guided us to a nearby wall and I slow winded him for two songs. I was so damn exhausted that my back was beginning to hurt. I straightened my back to press against his chest. I needed to catch my breath. He put his left hand on my stomach to push me further back so there was no space between us. Our bodies pressed against one another, back to chest, ass to crotch, I must admit I was becoming uneasy, but I was tired, I let it go for the moment. The guy lips touched my ear as he leaned in to whisper. He said, "You clean up nicely." It took me a minute to comprehend what he said because of the loud music. I turned around to get a view of him. Mystery intruder, even though the house was dim he's the most gorgeous man I've ever laid my eyes upon. His hazel eyes glistened, perfect smile, a slight gap between his two front teeth, his skin is a little darker than mine. He was dressed so fly, I remembered the red and yellow Polo shirt. To top off his image he has one little dimple resting in his right cheek. Damn, I'm one lucky girl if this is the guy that helped me. I smiled bashfully. He grabbed me by the waist, pulling me closer to him again. "I'm Rod," he managed to say above the music.

"LaSiah," I said into his ear. My mind was racing. I wished he hadn't seen me at my lowest like that, then again, I'm glad he did see me. If New Bern guys walking around looking like this, then I'm in trouble.

The music stopped, and the light flicked on. Kendra thanked everyone for coming out to meet us, but it was time to leave. This Rod and I locked eyes but didn't utter another word. He started to leave with the crowd, "See you around LaSiah," he said smiling.

CHAPTER 3

I awoke at three in the afternoon, that party tired me out. Good thing it's Saturday. I managed to unpack all my things, I even went to the superstore to get decorative pictures for the walls. I made the theme of my room giraffe print. I love some giraffes. My mom used to always tell the story of when Shae and I were two years old, we took a family trip to the zoo, and I stared at the giraffes longer than any animal. She said I used to always beg for her to take me back to see them. I'm glad I could find sheets, lamps, and rugs in the giraffe print. I even added my name to the wall in big pink letters, my favorite color. It did look weird with all the giraffe print, but who cares? As long as I like it. My room is now complete!

I called the hospital in Georgia to check on Kennon, but nothing has changed. I left a message with my favorite nurse, Sam. She knows and understands our situation. She has been his primary nurse since day one. Other nurses come to care for Kennon too, but they must report everything back to Sam. She has become like family to us. Over the past year and a half, she has made it her business to cook meals for Shae and me, and to also lend us her ear if we needed to vent. She was devasted when we broke the news to her about us moving, but she wished us the best. If I could have moved in with her I would've, but she's a cat lady and I am not.

Kendra and I prepared a slight dinner for the house. Spaghetti with meatballs, garlic bread, and a Caesar salad. I fixed myself an iced cold glass of water along with my dinner plate then headed to my room. I had a ton of tv shows to catch up on. Shae's ass is cooped up in her room with some nigga from the party. I swear her ass is so fucking easy. I rolled my eyes at the thought of what they were doing in there. I opted for a movie instead and ate my food. My mind ran off to that guy I danced with. You know how you see a sexy ass guy, and in your mind, you have already planned the entire future. Right now, Rod and I are married with three children…in my head. I'm truly not ready to be in a relationship, because I hate to have to tell him I'm a virgin. I hate that process because guys automatically assume I don't know anything about sex, and I do. I actually know a lot about sex, I just don't choose to partake in that activity just yet. I've never had a serious boyfriend because they always ended up breaking up with me, because I'm not hot in the ass. Most of the boys thought Aaron and I were in a relationship anyway. Either way, it didn't bother me, I like being single. I didn't have to answer to anyone, and I can do whatever I wanted without a nigga clocking my every move.

LaShae came into my room after her company left, and without knocking, "It looks good in here Siah!" She exclaimed, looking around. I blushed, proud of my/. work. "You're gonna have to come to help me with mine?"

I looked at her as if she were crazy, "No, you should've asked your company for help."

"Bitch don't be jealous because I got some last night," she said proudly.

"Jealous because you're a hoe?" I mumbled under my breath.

"What?!" She questioned, but she heard exactly what I said.

"Nothing," I laughed. This trick always acts like she scares some damn body. She's only five minutes older than me, she better check herself, "Who is he anyway?" I was curious.

"None of your damn business," she said as she marched out my room. She's mad now, I laughed, nobody told her to be so easy.

I finished eating my food before it got too cold, then I took my dirty dishes downstairs. I've always had the habit to keep dirty dishes, empty cans and bottles, and trash in my room, but I'm trying something new. Clean up as I go. I do want to know who LaShae fucked last night, she'll tell me in due time because she can't keep shit to herself.

I called Yazzy to see where she was at since she missed the party.

"Hello?" She answered.

"What happened to you last night?"

She took a long pause, "I was tied up, I heard it was jumping."

I rolled my eyes; this trick is on some other shit. It's cool though, I get so annoyed with females very easily which is why I rather befriend guys. Less drama and bullshit, "Well what are you doing now?"

Another long pause, "About to smoke with some friends, you should come over here." I looked at my attire, I wasn't dressed to go out nor did I want to, but I did want to see her. I got her new address, threw on something cute and headed out of the house. I unwrapped my hair in the car. Luckily, I don't have to travel far to her apartment, it's literally down the street. I applied my purple lipstick to my lips before I got out of the car. I didn't bother to knock on the door, she knew I was coming. It was two guys there when I stepped into her messy living room. Yazzy has always been a slob, but I can't understand how anybody can allow people in their homes when it's dirty like this. Clean the shit up first! I waved to everyone before I cleared a spot off so I could at least sit on the couch.

"Siah, these are my friends, Raymond and Chris. Y'all this is my girl Siah from Georgia." I waved again, they nodded their heads.

Chris started to roll up some weed. Raymond turned his attention to me saying, "I just left your spot."

I scrunched my face out of curiosity, "Yeah? You came to the party?"

"Yeah, and the after-party," he and Chris laughed...that annoyed me.

"Excuse me?" I said above their laughter.

"I chilled with your twin sister, Um...Shy."

"I think you mean Shae," the nigga fucked the girl, but don't know her name, damn shame.

"Yeah, yeah, yeah...that's it." Raymond isn't even that cute. I'm not the type of girl that goes off looks, but LaShae doesn't know him so she had to be looking at his appearance. So far, I'm not impressed by his personality either.

"She should've come," Yazzy spoke as she lit the blunt Chris previously rolled.

"She's busy," I lied. I hate sharing friends with LaShae, we've been doing it forever. Yazzy's back door flung open and it just about scared me to death. In walks Rod with two dudes in tow.

"What's goody, baby girl?" He said to Yazzy as he kissed her cheek. He dapped Chris and Raymond. "What's up?" He asked me as we locked eyes.

"Hey," I said softly. I was nervous, I was beginning to get hot.

"Rod, this is my friend Siah," Yazzy spoke.

He looked me over, up and down, "nice to meet you, Si." He licked his lips before sitting beside me. I started to get even more nervous, but he smelled good. "What's the move tonight Yaz?"

"Shit…this, smokin' and bullshittin'. What y'all got going on?" The two guys that came in with Rod stood at the door like they were bodyguards.

"You already know," they exchanged a look. Raymond extended his arm, trying to pass me the blunt he and Chris were smoking. I politely declined. "You don't smoke?" Rod asked me taking the blunt from Raymond.

"No, I don't," I proudly stated. Weed is not for me, don't get me wrong I've tried it, but I didn't get high so I'm good on it. I'll stick to my good ole bottle of rum.

"That's what's up, stay like that," he inhaled, blowing the smoke from his nostrils. He passed it to Yazzy, who already looked stoned. She sat next to Chris, she took a drag from the blunt and threw her head back. She blew the smoke straight up to the ceiling. I don't remember her being like this. From the condition of her house and the way they just lit up freely without asking her made me think this was a daily event in her life. I'm not sure how I feel about this right now. I said my goodbyes. Once outside I looked at my phone, missed calls from Kendra, Shae, and Aaron. I wasn't even in Yazzy's house for thirty minutes. The tap on my car window scared me half to death my phone dropped to the floorboard. I look to find out who the fuck almost made me shit my pants, it was Rod. I rolled the window down.

"Can I come?" He asked boldly with a grin on his face.

"Where?" I tried not to smile, but it's something about him that made that impossible.

"With you, wherever you're going," he licked his lips. I picked my phone up before I unlocked the car door. Rod climbed into the passenger seat. I glanced at him before I pulled off. I wonder about his bodyguards, and how he could just leave them like that. I also wonder about Yazzy being in the house with all those men, but I guess she can handle herself. I parked in my self-proclaimed parking spot. Peanut was asleep on the couch when we entered the house. More than likely he's drunk as a skunk and sleeping it off. I led the way to my room, once in, he immediately took his shoes off making himself comfortable on my bed. I sat across from the bed at my desk, "I like how you've changed it up in here."

"Thank you," I didn't have anything else to say. I find myself speechless around him. I watched as he examined every inch of my room.

"How you know Yaz?" he asked after a few moments passed.

"She's a childhood friend."

"Childhood? Naw yo, Yaz is like my little sister, I would've met you before."

"Maybe you weren't around when I came up here."

"I wish I had been," the look he gave me was everything, I melted. "You're from Georgia, right? What else can I learn about you?"

"Who says I want you to learn anything about me?"

He chuckled, "Is that the way to treat the man who took care of you last night?"

"Thank you for that by the way," I smiled. "But it's not much to learn. You know and have already butchered my name."

"So, I can't call you Si?"

"Nobody calls me that."

"Exactly. I don't like being like everybody else."

"I can see, but you can tell me about yourself. I mean you are the stranger in my house."

"I've probably been to this house more than you," he laughed.

"Have you?" I asked sarcastically.

"Peanut's my peoples," I rolled my eyes. It seems like everyone is his 'peoples'. "What you want to know?"

"Everything," I said while making myself comfortable in the computer chair.

He sat up, "Iight, name: Tyrrod Hill, aka Rod. 28. No Kids. Plenty of Money. What else?"

"Are you a good person?"

"Yeah," he nodded.

"How do you know?"

"What do you mean?" I could see he was beginning to become uneasy.

"I mean, do people tell you that you're a good person? I anticipated his answer.

"Nobody has to tell me I'm a good person. I don't look for others to justify me."

Good answer I thought to myself. He seems like the kind of guy that does his own thing. I decided at that moment that I can open up to him. "Well I'm 21 years old, currently a sophomore in college, I had a late start because I wanted to be sure college was for me. Honestly, I'm still deciding that." I laughed at myself for being so honest with him. I haven't told my sisters, but I think I'm going to drop out of college. I did transfer to the community college, maybe I will give it a chance. Only time will tell. "I'm a virgin and I like to take photos of everything. That's all you get for free."

"Woah, wait. You can't just speed pass, 'I'm a virgin', like that. What do you mean you're a virgin? Like a legit virgin?"

"Yes! Virgin as in I've never had sex, virgin," I said with as much attitude as possible. Maybe it was too early to let him know, but I didn't want him thinking we were gonna get down and dirty tonight. "Is that a problem?"

"Not for me. You don't meet too many virgins nowadays, I'm

shocked. You don't smoke, and you don't have sex. I like that," he smiled and that made me smile. I like an understanding type of guy. No, I didn't expect to be a virgin for so long, I'm not holding out until marriage. It just never happened for me, I had planned on losing it at sixteen, but it never happened so every year after that losing my virginity was the goal. Still, it never happened. I'm kind of glad it didn't because I saw so many girls in Georgia lose theirs to ain't shit niggas and end up hurt or tossed to their homeboys. I always said when I do lose it, I won't be throwing pussy at any- and everybody.

Rod and I continued to talk about everything, our families, our goals, silly things, we just talked enjoying each other's company. I learned that Raymond and Chris that were at Yazzy's house are his brothers, he has another brother named Quentin and a sister, Erica. He and his siblings live with their parents in an upscale development in Jamescity. He said he's always been drawn to the street life, and that's how he makes his money, but he does aspire to be a chef. A rich kid turned hood nigga who would have thought. By midnight I felt like I got a better sense of who Rod was as a person, and I can see myself liking him. His phone kept vibrating which annoyed me, but I didn't comment on it. If he wanted to talk to them, he would have answered. I felt pretty important. I was starting to get tired, so I joined him on the bed, I didn't want our conversation to end. I wrapped up in my fleece.

"Can I lay with you?" He asked and I nodded. I let him underneath the cover, I tensed up a little, "I'm not gonna touch you unless you want me to," he smiled.

"I believe you," and I did. This whole evening he has been a gentleman, so far he hasn't displayed any behavior of wanting to jump my bones. I closed my eyes and let my nose take in his scent. We laid face to face. Then I fell asleep.

I awoke at 6:24 am and Rod was gone. On the pillow he occupied last night was a small piece of paper with his name and number on it. I smelled the pillow, gosh, I love his scent. This Rod has left two lasting impressions on me, and I'm crushing on him hard. I've had crushes before, hell, I even had boyfriends before but none of them have been like Rod. I reached for my phone on my nightstand to call the number Rod left.

"Good morning, Si," he answered on the first ring.

I cleared my throat, "Good morning. I like how you left without saying bye."

"My bad, I had to handle some business and you were sleeping so peacefully I didn't want to wake you."

"I appreciate your consideration," I heard a loud moan coming from Shae's room which was next to mine, damn these thin walls. "Is your brother here?"

He laughed, "I don't know, why?"

"Whatever, you do know. My sister is in there moaning loud as hell."

He laughed again, "yeah, he's there. I needed a ride, so I borrowed his car since mine is still at Yazzy's. He wanted to stop by to say hi anyway."

I sighed loudly, I'm so tired of Shae and her shenanigans. "It's too early for this."

"I'm finishing up, so I can come back to get you. Are you hungry?"

"I can eat, I'll be ready soon," I showered and dressed, Shae and Raymond were still going at it when I went downstairs to wait for Rod. I started to bang on her damn door, but that'll be petty of me. Rod showed up minutes after I went outside, I gave him a small smile, but inside I was overjoyed. We told each other good morning again as I buckled my seat belt. We went to the diner literally up the street from my house. A small diner, but the interior was decorated beautifully. A retro diner with Pepsi-Cola all around. I remember when we first moved to Georgia, I was seven years old, my parents used to tell everyone they met about New Bern being the birthplace of Pepsi-Cola. Seeing this diner took me back. We sat in a booth and waited for our waitress to come to take our order. When she came over, she didn't look like she was having a good time, the attitude was written all over her face. Such a beautiful place, with a waitress with a chip on her shoulder. I hate when people go to work with an attitude, and it rubs off on everyone else. If you can't be one hundred percent, hell fifty percent happy then stay the fuck home. She took our order with an attitude, and to make matters worse she didn't even try to hide it. Normally, I wouldn't give my money to establishments with these kinds of workers, but then again, I wasn't paying. I ordered an omelet with waffles and a cup of coffee, Rod ordered a stack of pancakes, eggs, and bacon. I noticed the waitress was being extra rude when it came to my food, shit I was almost afraid to eat the food. "Do you know her?" I asked pointing to the waitress.

"Something like that, why do you ask?"

"Because it's clear it's a problem that I'm with you."

"I haven't noticed."

"Well I have and I'm uncomfortable with her as my waitress, she's rude as hell and I don't like it. Actually, I'm ready to go back home." I said as serious as possible. "Is she one of your hoes?" That would explain her behavior toward me.

"Naw, she ain't nobody," he poured syrup over his pancakes.

"You sure?" I slid my plate to the side, it's no chance in hell I was eating this food.

"I don't have hoes, just bitter exes." He smiled at me, but I wasn't amused.

"Bitter?" Rod is fine and all, but I don't want nor need any unnecessary drama with bitches I don't know. "Can you take me home?" I asked, maintaining my cool. Between this waitress bitch and him asking like he didn't notice her mood aggravated me to the fullest.

"Why? You haven't touched your food."

"I'm ready to go," I gathered my purse.

"Why?" He stared at me, "because of her?" He pointed towards the waitress. I didn't say anything. "Aye," he called out to her, motioning her to come to our table. She came over promptly with the same attitude. "Yo, your attitude is fucked up and it's upsetting my date, I wanna talk to your manager."

"Are you serious Rod?" She asked, quickly dropping the attitude, I glared at her. She started to become nervous.

"Dead fucking serious, that shit ain't cool yo," he was so mad at this point and it was sexy as hell. I've never been a confrontational type of chick, but I can get used to somebody taking up for me.

"I can lose my job," she whined.

"Well drop the fucking attitude," she nodded in agreement then started to walk away. "Oh yeah, apologize to her too yo," he said to her.

"I'm sorry…" She stopped, anticipating my name, I told her, "I'm sorry, LaSiah." I could tell she wanted to say something else, but her best bet was to keep her mouth closed. I still wanted to go home, and I told him that. Fuck that food. He got the bitch to box the food up and to bring the check. He paid the bill and even left the bitch a twenty-dollar tip. I completely understand common courtesy, but she didn't deserve a single penny, but that's his money. I didn't speak or look at him the entire ride back to my house, I got out without so much of a goodbye. I liked the fact he finally said something to her about her attitude, but that apology was so disingenuous. But leaving her a tip pretty much tells her that her attitude was acceptable. I marched into the house, up the steps, and into my room. I'm mad at myself for not letting the thought of this fine ass nigga having hoes cross my mind.

Shae came into my room smiling, "So…you and Raymond's brother, Rod?" She questioned.

I shook my head. I didn't want to talk to her about it. She got the picture and went back to her room. Shae and I never talk about each other's relationships or the lack thereof. Her mind always goes to sex when I start talking to a guy, but she needs to understand that I will make that decision on my own. Sex is not everything. I can't think about any of that right now, her or Rod. I start classes tomorrow and I don't need to be distracted by a nigga anyway. I deleted his number from my phone. Fuck it.

I only have two classes today, I was going to go job hunting, but I've decided to hold out on that right now. I must focus on school. I finalized my class schedule with my advisor and luckily, I was able to only have classes on Mondays and Wednesdays. I sat in class ready to learn about African American literature. I love history and literature, especially when it's about my people. I was minding my own business when two skinny chicks sat in the desks beside and in front of me.

"Hey, you're Rod's girl, right?" The darker complexed one asked.

I looked at her sideways. I thought to myself, 'here we go again', and responded with, "and you are?"

"I'm his sister, Erica, and that's" she pointed to the brown-skinned girl on my right, "is my best friend, Drea." She extended her hand to me. I shook it to be nice. "It's nice to meet you, to put a face to the name."

"I'm not his girl by the way," I corrected her. Rod and I have only been on one date if you can call it that, and now people think I'm his girl.

"That's the word around town," Drea chimed in. I now know why they call this town News Bern.

"Well my brother doesn't take up for anybody and the word on the street is he told Taylor about herself yesterday." I rolled my eyes at her last statement. Did he put her up to this? He knows he blew his chance. After class, these bitches were still up on my ass. "LaSiah, right?" Erica was steadily asking questions.

"Yup," I replied nonchalantly, I wanted them to hear the irritation in my voice.

"Where is your twin? Does she go here too?" Drea questioned. Why are they so pressed about me and Shae? Shae was supposed to take classes, but she claims she needs a break, but that's none of their concern. I ignored her question.

"Do you want to grab lunch with us? We're going to this pizza place right up the road," Erica said.

I finally reached my car, "Raincheck? I have plans with my friend, Yazzy."

"Yazzy?" They looked at each other and laughed like hyenas. Childish.

"I'll see y'all, next class," before I went to Yazzy's house I grabbed us a couple of cheeseburger meals. "Yazzy?" I called out through the screen door. She opened the door looking way better than she did the other night. Plus, her house was clean. I kicked my shoes off. When your house is clean, I feel more comfortable. We ate our lunch and watched a movie.

Yazzy is a girl that knows what she wants in life and goes after it.

She's always been independent, I guess that comes from being raised by a single mother. We met one summer at a camp, the local recreation center, also known as the gym. She was tough and sassy, and I loved it. We used to take weekly field trips to the skating ring and on one day this girl wanted to be big and bad, showing off for the boys. She pushed me as I was skating backward. I fell so hard my knee bruised. Yazzy helped me up, but that was after she punched the girl in her face. From that moment on, we've been friends. She became my diary when I needed to vent. We used to talk about moving to Greensboro together, but things fell through. Distance made us closer and she confided in me when she'd gotten pregnant at sixteen. She ended up having an abortion after she cried and begged me to help her pay for it. I sent her half of the money that I saved from my allowance. I didn't agree with her decision, but she's my friend so I supported her. To this day we don't mention it. I don't think her mother knows about the abortion, she has an aunt who is five years older than us, she signed the necessary papers for her. It's a secret between all of us.

She lit a blunt after we finished our lunch. Raymond, Chris, and Rod walked into her house. I tensed up. I didn't want to see his ass, I spoke to them though. I grabbed my phone to play my game, I needed my attention elsewhere, so I won't look at his sexy face. Now looking more closely at Raymond, I retract my statement because he is a cutie, and I can see why Shae is fucking with him. His pecan brown complexion, soft brown eyes, waves, and a smile complimented him. Chris has the lightest skin tone, and although he's the youngest, he's the tallest. They all favor each other a lot but Rod is by far the finer one.

"What are y'all about to do?" Yazzy asked the brothers. Raymond sat beside Yazzy, Chris sat beside me, and Rod stood. He was burning a hole in the side of my face. I felt it, but I kept my eyes on my phone.

"About to go to the gym," Raymond answered.

"Y'all wanna come?" Chris asked.

"Hell yeah," Yazzy said before I could utter a word. I cut my eyes at her. I hate when people answer for me, now I feel like I obligated to go even though I didn't want to. All I know is, I'm not driving to be wasting my gas on bullshit. I tried not to show the attitude that I just developed. I do want to be likable in this new town. We all rode in Rod's dark blue SUV and guess where I was forced to sit...on the passenger side. I don't think none of them knows that we aren't on speaking terms. We met, we talked, and that's it. Nothing more, nothing less. Yazzy and I grabbed a seat on the bleachers, and all eyes were on us. I figured she gets the stares all the time because she strides without worry. The brothers dressed down in their gym shorts and white t-shirts. Why did they have to do that? My eyes were instantly glued to Rod's muscular body. They played full court of basketball with some other guys who were also hanging out at the gym. Rod has a little attitude on him, he kept getting frustrated because his teammates weren't playing as hard as he was. Talking shit to all of them. At one moment I thought he and Raymond were going to throw blows. I just watched him in awe. The boys rested for a little after the first game was over. Rod sat in front of me and leaned back in between my legs like I gave him permission.

"Can you massage my shoulders?" He requested, and I obliged. I touched his sweaty back, rubbing my hands over his shoulders. He was so warm and soft. "We need to talk too yo." I didn't respond, I kept massaging him. We left the gym at 6:30 p.m. It was low-key fun watching them getting sweaty playing basketball. Despite all the eyes, I swear these people in this town are nosey as fuck. We stopped for milkshakes before going back to Yazzy's apartment. I slurped on my Oreo Cheesecake milkshake. I needed to make my way home. They were about to smoke anyway, and I didn't want to be around that. When I got home, I showered then finished off my milkshake. I contemplated on giving Mr. Hill another chance. Maybe I was being a little judgmental and childish about the situation. Honestly, I can't expect a guy like Rod to not have bitches he used to fuck with look at me sideways. I mean look at me, I'm cute as hell. I have enjoyed the times Rod and I have spent with each other, and I do want to get to know him on a deeper and personal level. I'm intrigued by him, and who knows he just might be the one...the only one to steal LaSiah Martin's heart.

CHAPTER 4

A light knock awoke me from my sleep, I don't sleep heavy, so a pin dropping could wake me up. I rubbed my eyes as the door slowly crept open. It was Rod. I sat up and looked at him in the darkness, the moonlight was hitting his face so good. He sat on the foot of my bed.

"My bad for showing up so late, Shae let me and Raymond in," he took off his shoes.

"It's fine," I cleared my throat. I made a mental note to thank my twin. It had to be at least 3:00 a.m.

"You not fucking with me no more?"

"What's makes you say that?" I yawned.

"You've been very stand-offish yo. You left out the car after breakfast without a thank you. I've never been so disrespected."

"Disrespected? I'll admit it was distasteful of me for not thanking you for the meal, but I was so thrown off by that ex of yours." I reached over to my nightstand to turn on my table lamp.

"I never said she was my ex," he looked at me.

"Didn't you though? You said you have bitter exes."

"Yeah, I do, but she's just a friend to one. Females love to hate a nigga that's not fucking with their friends anymore. I got exes, but what nigga don't? I'm trying to get with you, so I'm not worrying about anybody else." I beamed inside although I kept a straight face. To be quite frank, I do like this dude and it is way too early for us to be having these types of problems. I would like to see how far this thing between us can go.

"I did appreciate breakfast," I said sweetly.

"I'm glad," he smiled that smile. "Are you interested?"

"In what?"

"Me? Because I'm interested in you."

I rolled my eyes playfully, "I guess you can say I'm a little interested," I joked. Hell, who am I fooling? I'm a lot interested. We laid side-by-side, I turned on a movie then turned off the lamp. I drifted off to sleep. When I awoke, Rod was behind me with his hand was on my stomach. I stirred, but he held me tighter.

"Good Morning," he whispered into my ear.

"Good Morning to you," I smiled. I've never had sleepovers with a guy. Mostly because I was afraid of what would happen during the late night. But with Rod, I feel safe, although I'm just getting to know him, I feel like I can trust him to keep his hands to himself.

"What you got to do today?"

"Nothing," I yawned as I turned to see his beautiful face.

"We can chill all day then, I ain't got shit to do either," the smell of his morning breath hit me, but I didn't mind it. "Is that cool with you?"

I nodded. "Excuse me for a second," I reached for my phone, I called to check on Kennon. Sam said that the doctors are observing him since they've lifted him from the coma. Scans are showing no signs of swelling in his brain, but he still has a long road ahead of him. I felt emotional about Kennon's situation, but I can't let Rod see that side of me. I nestled my head in his chest, he wrapped his arms around me. "What do you like in girls?" I asked him to change the mood.

"I like somebody like you."

I laughed at him, trying to run the game on me, "Really? How am I?"

"You're smart, family-oriented, you have potential, and that attitude of yours is growing on me."

"*My attitude?*" We shared a laugh.

"What do you look for in a man?"

"Well I've never really dated, but I'll take honesty, trust, genuine love, and respect. I've just seen friends and family go through a lot with men, and I just want to be treated right. I don't want to question a guy's love for me. I want him to make me feel secure," I spoke honestly. I grew up watching my parents interact with each other, the love they had for one another was so great, it was contagious. Even after an argument, love was still in the air.

"I can be that man for you," I smiled as he stroked my cheek. He *could* be that one for me."

Shae barged into my room it scared us both, we broke our embrace. She came bearing two plates of pancakes, eggs, and bacon. Raymond was behind her carrying two big cups of orange juice. "Ray and I cooked breakfast, and we thought about y'all," she announced.

"Appreciate it," Rod said for the both of us. Shae's ass does not cook, I don't know what Raymond is doing to her, but I hope he keeps it up. She looks happier too. Shae is the type that walks around hating the world. She's pretty much unapproachable and not friendly until you get to know her. She didn't have a boyfriend back in Georgia, but she did date…a lot. I don't think she's found what she wants in a man yet. This new behavior is incredible, she does need some happiness in her life, hopefully, Raymond can give her that. After our parents died, she totally checked out. She barely ate, slept, and she locked herself in her room all day. My behavior was the same, but I needed her to lean on and she wasn't there. I had to handle everything with the house like making the mortgage payments on time, the light bill, and insurance. Luckily, our cars are paid for. Shae would slide her debit card under her room door. I picked myself up, I clung to Kennon. I visited him every day, talked to him like he could hear me, and I cried to him as well. During this time is really when I became close to Sam. Shae didn't go visit Kennon often, I can count on one hand how many times she went to see him. I didn't nag her about it, because visiting him was *my* safe place. She came out of her funk after a year, but it was still hard for both of us, then we had to make the decision to move.

I got ready after breakfast. Rod said he wanted to take me out to tour the city. Although I know everything there is to know about this city, I agreed. I would love to see his view of New Bern. We first stopped in The Bricks, my father used to talk about this neighborhood all the time. He strictly forbade us from stepping foot in it when we used to visit during the summer. But Kendra always took us, and Daddy never found out. I've met some of the realest people in The Bricks, but I doubt if they remember me now.

"This is my hood," he informed me, "I am here every day, I love this place. The good, the bad, and the ugly." I nodded my head as I soaked in the information. Daddy said only thugs hung in The Bricks, but Rod doesn't seem like a thug. "So, when I'm not with you, I'm here with my niggas," I smiled. The next stop was in The Woods, a neighborhood remarkably similar to The Bricks but not as rough. Yazzy lives in The Woods, and a good bit of my family stays here as well. "This is my other hood. Only if I'm at Yazzy's spot is when I'm here, and I got niggas living out here too." I nodded again. I wonder how many friends he has. We rode down one of the main streets in New Bern, and it has changed. I noticed little things on my first drive here, but now I see it all, and the improvements are amazing. We drove to Jamescity, after all the ridiculous traffic we pulled in front of a brick two-story house with a huge wooden door. The entirety of the home was gated, he punched in the numeric code to open the gate. Clearly, this is his home. I noticed a garden sectioned off in the front of the yard.

"Stomping ground?" I questioned, already knowing the answer to my question.

"Home sweet home," he sang. He unbuckled his seat belt. "Are you ready to meet my folks?" He smiled. I stared at him like he was crazy. It's way too soon to be meeting his parents. I need to get to know him better. I could feel my palms getting sweaty, and it felt like sweat beads were dropping from my face. "I'm just bullshittin', they're not home," he laughed. I guess nervousness was written all over my face. We exited the car and I entered the house cautiously. This home was beautiful inside and out. From the cherry wood flooring to the pastel-colored walls. We took our shoes off at the door, placing them on the shoe rack nearby. I noticed the floral drapes in the living room, also above the fireplace was a family portrait. I stared at the photo, admiring the features of each person. His mother is stunning, and Rod looks like his father. A brown leather sectional occupied the living room along with a glass coffee table. There was a 75-inch television in the room, and a giant fish tank filled with goldfish. The shag carpet felt amazing under my feet. Other photos of Rod and his siblings invaded the walls. I took in every square inch of the room. Rod led us up the black and white carpeted stairs.

"Ray?" Erica called from the end of the hallway.

"Naw, it's me," Rod said, she peeped from the room door. I stood behind him so her childish ass didn't see me.

"Oh, hey! Where's Ray?"

"He's out, what's up, Erica?"

"Nothing," she rolled her eyes. "Ma said don't be having nobody in her house."

He laughed, "she said that shit to you, not me."

"The same rules apply to you," she rolled her neck. I rolled my eyes as I stepped from behind him. She's a pesky little bitch. "Oh, hey LaSiah," her tone changed quickly, she sounded happy to see me.

"Hey," I faked a smile, "I really have to use the bathroom," I tugged on his arm to add effect. We left her standing in the hallway looking stupid as hell.

His room was not only big but clean as hell. It was simply decorated. A huge picture of himself hung over the bed, this guy is completely full of himself, but I like it. He sat on his king-sized bed after showing me to the bathroom, which was decorated in all red. I tinkled then headed back into his room. I sat on his tan-colored recliner that overlooked the backyard. Underground pool and another garden. This garden had two chairs and a table in the middle of it. A barbeque pit to the left of the yard along with brown wicker furniture set on the side of the pool. The cushions in the seats were purple. It looked very relaxing out there. With a home like this, I can't understand why he likes to be in the hood. This dude has top of the line stuff in his house and his bedroom. I admired his portrait, it looked painted, and it's incredibly beautiful. He's exceptionally beautiful. We didn't have much to talk about, my attention was on his exquisite home. He went into his bathroom to take a shower, it's funny how quickly we are getting comfortable with each other. I really like and appreciate that he hasn't tried anything sexual. I can let my wall down with him. I can say these last couple of days in New Bern, I've opened up a lot compared to in Georgia. All the feelings I'm feeling for Rod right now is new to me, I don't know how to even begin to sort them out.

He came from the shower without a shirt, only his gym shorts graced his body. The water beads glistened off his chest. Why did he have to come out like that? My eyes traveled up and down his body. His six abs begged for my attention, and I was giving them my undivided. I bit my bottom lip. All sorts of thoughts began to flow through my mind. He dried his chest then put on a white t-shirt. He reached in the dresser beside his bed to pull out a small box before he sat down. A sack of weed was in the box along with a grinder and a pack of cigarillos. I watched him as he ground a portion of the weed, split the cigarillo down the middle and discarded the guts in a small corner store bag. He began the rolling process, he licked the cigarillo with so much precision that it turned me on. He immediately sparked it up, he laid back on his bed as the smoke invaded his lungs, I could tell this was his peace, and for a split second, I wanted to feel that peace. I too, wanted to escape to a different place. With each puff, he slipped into his tranquility. I took my eyes from him and returned them to the backyard view. It reminded me of my house back in Georgia. My father used to keep a garden, it calmed him, and he used to let me help him a lot. I enjoyed that time out there with Daddy, only him and I. We only grew vegetables and fruits, Daddy was always a stickler with money so anything that helped him save a penny, he was all for.

"What are you thinking about over there?" Rod asked, interrupting my thoughts.

"Nothing," I turned to him smiling. I noticed he had completed the blunt.

"Why you all the way over there? Come over here," his eyes were low. "What do you want to do next?" He asked as I propped myself on his pillows, he turned over to look at me.

"Questions," I said a bit too cheery.

"Not again," he rolled his eyes playfully. "Naw, what's up?"

"Being that you're always in either The Bricks or The Woods what kind of things have you seen?"

"Shit, I've seen it all. Aunts and uncles turned into crackheads, cousins fucking for fast food, and one time this nigga laced Chris' weed." I was in disbelief, especially by the last statement. I've always thought when someone got laced they lose their mind, and as far as I can see nothing is wrong with Chris. "I had to beat the nigga ass that did that shit, shit's crazy. I'm not well-liked, but I'm damn sure respected. I don't play about my brothers or sister," I liked that because I'm the same way about my siblings. Only I can talk shit about them or chastise them…nobody else. "Can I ask you a question?" He asked and I nodded. "Why haven't you had sex? I mean you're beautiful and any man in his right mind would've given you the business."

"Truthfully, I don't know. It just never happened, and it got to the point that I didn't care if it did or not. I'm happy either way."

"I feel you, so you haven't done anything?"

"Hmm…Yeah, I've done the basics, kissing mostly," I answered. Truth be told, this conversation was getting to be a little too much. A guy has never really asked me that question. He eyed me, "how many girls have you slept with?"

He laughed loudly and I was trying to find the humor, "does it matter?"

"Well, if you want to be my friend then no, but if you want to be more then yeah," I said sternly I may have jumped the gun thinking he even wanted more than a friendship from me. I hope he wants to be more because I want him to be more than a friend.

He stopped laughing and gazed towards the window, "I've hit a lot of bitches, and I don't count. The only time numbers mean anything to me is when I'm counting my money."

I rolled my eyes at his answer, but I'll accept it…for now. Shit, with the way he looks he probably sexed many of the bitches in New Bern. I didn't want to ask him any more questions if I'm not gonna get the answers I seek. I played with my phone. I sent a text to Aaron. I'm so used to talking to him every day, but I've been so focused on Rod. We sat in silence for a minute or two, a text from Aaron came in. He was at work and was going to call me later.

"Over fifty," Rod said.

"Huh?" I said, looking over my phone. I knew exactly what he was talking about. How does one fuck over fifty girls? I barely even know fifty bitches.

"I think I've done hit over fifty hoes," I shook my head. This is a major turn off, I can understand ten girls, but fifty? Damn.

"Did you love any of them?"

"I love all females," he chuckled, but I was serious as a heart attack. "No, seriously."

He sighed deeply, "I really don't know, maybe two of them."

"Only two?"

"I'm a man Si. I used to fuck those who wanted to be fucked. I'm not like that no more." I rolled my eyes, how do I know? Rod's a man-whore, but why don't I really care? I admit, it is a turn-off, but I can deal, right?

"Promise that part of you is in the past?"

He smiled, "I promise. Honestly, I would've tried to have sex with you by now. I normally don't lie next to females and not fuck."

"Well, I'm a different type of female."

"I see, and I like it," I blushed. "Have you ever been in love?"

"Never."

"Why?"

I shrugged my shoulders. I didn't have an answer for him. I guess guys back in Georgia didn't find me dateable or wife-able. I've never met any guy who wanted to wait for a virgin to decide to have sex. "The whole sex thing I would presume," I found the words to say.

"Them Georgia niggas are fools, I've only known you for a couple of days and you're worth the wait." I smiled, this could've been the universe's way of saving me for Rod. What if he's my soulmate? Love at first sight shit? I stared at him, I like the way his goatee decorated his face, so full and jet black. His lips look so damn juicy, I long for the day to kiss him. I wonder if he could feel me staring at him, but I can't help myself.

He got dressed, and then we left his beautiful home. We grabbed something to eat before going to Yazzy's house. I would have rather stayed at his house but in due time. Yazzy's house is cool too. Chris and Raymond were there, as usual, but I was surprised to see Shae. They were all smoking on a blunt when we walked in. I can't believe Shae calls herself smoking weed. I'm the only one in this apartment not high. I feel so out of place. I should loosen up just a little bit and smoke. No, Rod says he likes that I don't smoke. I can't be like those other girls he has dealt with. I watched t.v. as they reached their high, it was four blunts in rotation. I covered my nose that way I didn't catch a contact. It's so annoying being around people who do that shit you don't do, it's not fun. I'm not against anyone getting high, but damn be considerate.

"I'll be back, I'm going to get some air," I said, but I doubt if they heard me because they were too busy cackling. I sat on the hot porch step, it burned the back of my thighs slightly, but anything was better than being in there.

"What's wrong?" I turned around to see Rod. This dude moves fast, I didn't even hear him approach me.

"Nothing really, I don't like being around all that smoke."

"Why didn't you say something?"

"Well, I thought the coughing would've been a sign. You can go ahead and finish, I'm good out here."

"Naw," he protested, "let's walk." He grabbed my hand to help me up from the porch. We walked hand in hand down the streets. The Woods is closer to the downtown area and waterfront, the view at this time of the day was beautiful, the sun beaming off the river. I can get used to this, my type of romance. We walked until the sun went down talking and laughing. Is it wrong of me to be thinking that I'm falling for this guy and it's only been three days? Is that even possible? If it's not oh well because at this point, I'm ready to give dude everything I got. The connection between us is extraordinarily strong, and I know he feels it too.

Raymond and Shae were gone when we got back to Yazzy's house. We chilled with her and Chris for a while before Rod drove me home in Chris' Lexus. They switch cars like it's nothing. Shae knows not to touch my car and I know not to touch hers. He parked in front of my house, reached over to take my hand into his. "Can I stay with you tonight?" He asked, but I hope by now he knows that he doesn't have to ask, I nodded, "Iight, I gotta make a couple of stops and I'll be right back."

"Okay," I smiled, "I'll leave the door unlocked for you," he kissed my hand before I got out the car.

I prepared myself for bed and watched a movie as I waited for Rod's arrival. I hope those stops don't take too long because I have class in the morning and I'm not trying to be late. I dozed off and awoke at 3:49 a.m. No Rod. No phone calls. One thing that pisses me off is when someone lies to me. It's annoying. If he wasn't going to come back, say that, don't get my hopes up. I guess he's not into me like I'm into him, I'm a fucking idiot for thinking I could have a fairy tale romance. I sent him a simple text saying, 'Good Night!" then I powered my phone off. He's not my man, and I don't want him to know I'm upset with him. Fuck him. I have a class in a couple of hours.

CHAPTER 5

I couldn't even concentrate in class. My mind kept roaming to Rod. Why would he stand me up like that last night? The only conclusion I got was he was with somebody else. Let me find out who the fuck she is and I'm going to introduce myself just to let her know how her man has been in my face and in my bed since we've met. I can't stand a lying ass nigga. I left the school mad as hell, and for no reason. He doesn't even have the decency to call me to apologize, I'm over him. I went home, cleaned my room then took a much-needed nap.

I slept until the next morning, and before I could wipe the crust from my eyes Shae burst into my room.

"You don't have class today right?" She asked, standing over me, I hate when people do that.

"No, why?" I yawned.

"Rod wants to see you."

I sighed, "He has my damn number."

"Actually, he doesn't. His phone was stolen last night, so he asked Ray to get up with me so I could let you know."

"No, I don't want to see him," I shook my head.

"Why not?" She looked disappointed.

"Because I don't," I said with attitude, I meant what I said, Fuck him!

"Come on, Siah. This could be good for you. You're trying to shut him out just like you did to every boy in Georgia that was interested in you."

I rolled my eyes, "I. don't. want. to. see. him. Relay that message,"

31

she stormed out my room, that bitch can't make me see somebody I don't want to see. Talking about his phone was stolen. Whatever! Was his car stolen too? Because he could have easily stopped by the house, let me calm myself down and get on with my day. I want to take a trip to this mall.

I rode down Martin Luther King Boulevard with my hair flying in the wind. It's a nice day out, not too hot like the Georgia heat. I purchased three outfits, two pairs of sandals and some giraffe pictures. It wasn't a lot of shops to choose from in the mall, but I made out surprisingly good. I left the mall, grabbed a cookies and cream ice cream cone then went to chill out at a local park. I watched the small children play. They were so full of life. I smiled as one fell and another stopped to help him up. My phone rung breaking me from that moment, it was Yazzy.

"What's up Yazzy?"

"Where are you at?" She sounded antsy.

"The park, what's up?"

"Come to my house."

"For what? What's up?" I was getting annoyed with her. She's too close to Rod, and he probably told her to call me. Such a coward.

"Just come now please, damn." She disconnected the call. She really got me bent.

I showed up at her house twenty minutes later, I finished my ice cream first. "Yazzy?" I called when I noticed she wasn't in her kitchen or living room.

"I'm back here," she called from the back. I went down her hallway, searching for her. She was laying on her junky ass bed. When I entered the room she sat up, cleared a space for me to sit. I noticed she had something clenched in her hand, and she looked stressed. "I have something to tell you, but you have to promise not to repeat it to anyone."

"I never do," she handed me what was in her hand. A pregnancy test, I didn't know what to say. The two little lines indicated a positive result. She started to cry, and it instantly got weird for me. I'm not the comforting type, I try my best, but it always feels awkward to me.

"How am I gonna explain this to Q?"

First, who the hell is Q? I've never seen a nigga over here by the name of Q. Hell, I didn't know she was involved with anybody. "What do you mean? And who is Q?"

"Quentin, my man. I've told you about Si," I don't remember I just nodded. "But this isn't his baby. It's Chris'."

So, this tramp has been fucking Chris? No wonder he's always here, "Okay, let's start over," I said to her, handing the test back. "Remind me who Q is again?" I know he's her man, but this scary look on her face frightened me, so I can tell he's more.

"He's their brother."

"Who's brother?" I was confused.

"Oh, my...you act so fucking lost at times. I have to break everything down to you. Damn!"

"Bitch, you called me here, I can leave." I pointed towards the door.

"Calm down, my emotions are high right now," she said changing her attitude. "Q...is Quentin, he's Ray, Rod, and Chris' older brother."

Now I remember Rod saying something about Quentin. I haven't met him yet and Rod hasn't said much about him. This just makes me feel stupid all over again, here I am ready to give Rod my all and I don't know everything about him. "Rod doesn't talk about him like he talks about Raymond and Chris."

"That's because they're going through it right now," she explained in so many words, but whatever. I don't care. I don't have intentions of seeing Rod again.

"So, you're fucking brothers?" I judged, only because that shit is trifling.

"Chris just happened. A lot. What am I going to do?"

"Are you sure it's Chris' baby?"

"Yes. Q's been in jail for the past six months," she started to cry again. Bitches like her, I don't have sympathy for. Bitches like her love to fuck multiple niggas then look stupid when they get caught up.

"I don't know what to tell you but to be honest with all the parties involved. How did you and Chris hook up anyway?" I curiously asked.

"It just happened. He has a little girlfriend too. I don't think I'm ready for a child right now," she cried harder.

It took everything in me not to laugh in her face, because she's feeding me bullshit. I know Yazzy and she'd be inconsolable if this wasn't what she wanted. Thinking back to that day when I received the phone call from her. She was crying so hard I couldn't make out her words. She was hurt, confused, and scared; I could tell it in her voice. But now, now she's happy, I can sense a small bit of fearfulness too, but overall, this bitch is ecstatic. I'm not quite sure if it's because she wants Chris or the money the family has. I don't care, I'll let her do her. "Congratulations," I said snidely, disregarding her last statement.

"Yo...Yaz?" Raymond's voice boomed through the apartment. I silently prayed Rod wasn't with him. She quickly dried her face before going to greet him. I exhaled deeply before following her. We sat in the living room as usual. Luckily, it was only Raymond visiting. Is it a day that goes by that they don't come over here? If it's not one of them, it is all. She loves the attention too. I examined my hands, and my nails were hit. They desperately screamed for a manicure. While Yazzy and Raymond were engaged in some random conversation, I excused myself.

"Where are you going?" She asked.

"To a nail shop, I need a mani pedi as soon as possible. Would you like to come to take your mind off of what's happening?"

"Hell yeah, I need this. Ray, watch my house." She put on her shoes before he could even agree or protest. I drove us to Jamescity, I noticed a nail shop that day I went out with Rod. Jamescity has come up a lot, and it has more businesses now than I remember. The nail shop was clean, and the staff was friendly. We got our pedicures first. Their tiny hands felt so good on my feet. If I could, I would pay her to massage my feet all day. I chose cerise, a form of pink, for my fingers and toes. I don't like having false nails, tips, or whatever you want to call them. I stick with a gel overlay. Yazzy got the tips and she got them long, with ratchet ass colors and designs on each nail, but to each its own. My nail technician finished my nails fast, and I had to wait on Yazzy. I was completely dry when I reached for my debit card to pay for the services.

"No, no," the Asian man said to me.

I was confused, what the fuck he means no. I hope he didn't think I was paying for Yazzy's too, "Excuse me?"

"Young man pay. Young man pay for you."

"Huh? What man?" He pointed out the window. I rolled my eyes when I saw it was Rod. He was leaning against his car. I thanked the man.

"Thank you," I said to Rod when I went outside. I folded my arms.

"Not a problem at all," he said charmingly. "What's up though? Did you get my message?"

"Oh yeah, I got it," I answered him with attitude.

He frowned, "What's wrong?"

"Nothing, I gotta be back to Yazzy," I turned to walk away, but he grabbed my arm gently. My mind said pull away, but my body melted at his touch. I turned to face him as he drew me closer to him. He wrapped his arms around my waist. We stared into each other's eyes for a moment contemplating our next move.

"Can I take you somewhere to talk?" He asked, his hands moved closer to my butt.

"I have to take Yazzy back home."

"Leave her your car," I looked at him like he was crazy. "I'll leave her mine." He went inside the nail shop to give his car keys to Yazzy. I sat in my car waiting for him like a puppy waiting for its owner to return. I like his nerve thinking he can pop up on me any time he wants. "I'm driving," he said when he returned.

I shook my head, "I don't let anyone drive my car."

"Come on, live a little." I exhaled before climbing to the passenger seat. He took off, sometime later we were at the beach in Morehead City. I've missed this beach. I got my first seashell from this beach. We walked hand in hand, with our feet in the sand, my freshly painted toes stepping into the warm sand. He took off his black shirt to lay it on the sand so I could sit. I took in the view of the beach, the cloudless blue sky, the tan sand, and the people at play. Rod arm draped around my shoulders, "I love how you get lost in your surroundings."

I smiled, "I like to appreciate the moments of life." He pulled out a phone from his shorts and placed it in his lap, "I thought it was stolen."

"It's a new one," he laughed stealthily. "My phone was stolen, I don't lie about stupid shit Si."

"Whatever you say," I continued to look out over the ocean.

"That's the problem? Yo, if I could've made it over last night I would've. Shit got crazy. I'm trying to make it up to you," I grinned inside.

"What happened last night?"

He sighed, "I went to my homeboy's house, and…" he sighed again, but this time deeply. "My ex was there," he was tensing up. Just spit it out, I thought. I'm not your girl. I don't know why it's so hard for niggas to tell the truth. I waited for his response. "We were getting lit, one thing led to another. Then I realized my phone was missing and she had it." At this point in the story, I was over his explanation. I was up all night and he wanted to have a fling with an ex. "Long story short, she got pissed when she saw your text, so she left with my shit."

I laughed harder than I intended to. I have two options; leave him alone or continue to make these bitches mad. I grabbed his new phone from his lap, "What's your lock code?"

He smiled, "My birthday," I typed in 0105, it unlocked. I went to the camera then started to take mad selfies of myself and some of us together. I set the perfect one as his lock and home screen and then gave it back to him. Give that ex something else to hate on. He smiled as he admired the picture. The sun was beginning to set, he got behind me, and I rested my head on his chest. He wrapped his arms around me again, I didn't care that the sand was covering my legs if I was in his arms. The breeze from the ocean brushed my skin. His phone rang, he looked at it then powered it off. "I want you to myself," he whispered into my ear. The raspy in his voice gave me chills. He kissed my earlobe making a trail of kisses down my neck. I shivered. My neck is my spot, one kiss and waterfalls. I closed my eyes as I leaned over to give him more access. He gently bit and suckled on my neck. A light moan escaped me. His hand slipped underneath my shirt and sports bra. A warm sensation overcame me as he cupped my bare breast in his big hand. Our breathing increased, I wanted to stop it all, but I enjoyed the feeling. But we're moving too fast, right? He rubbed his fingertips across my hard nipples. His tongue swirled on my neck almost like he was writing his name. "Let's go," he whispered. He helped me up. I grabbed his shirt, shook the sand out of it, and then I put it on. It smelt of him. The ride back to New Bern was a silent one on my end. We listened to the music he liked, he rapped the lyrics to himself. We held hands the entire ride, "Your house or mine?"

"What makes you think this date isn't over?"

He smirked, "Iight." He parked my car right behind his car when we reached Yazzy's house. Shae's car was parked across the street. We sat in the car silent for a while. Maybe he was mad at me for making that comment, but I was joking. Then again, most people can't take my jokes. "Yours or mine?" he asked again.

"Mine. I need to take my stuff home."

"Iight, I'll meet you there," he followed me back to my house and even helped with my bags. Kendra and Peanut were watching a movie downstairs, we spoke to them before we headed to my room. I put my phone on its charger then placed the shopping bags in the closet. I'm a little nervous to be around him right now. I don't want him thinking we could do more than what we did on the beach. He removed his shoes then laid on my bed. I excused myself to the bathroom. I needed to touch up the garden just in case he wants to play in it. Rod was on the phone when I returned to the room, my phone at that. He had a smug look on his face. He ended the call but kept my phone in his hand. "Aaron called," he said with a whiff of jealousy in his voice.

I took my phone from him, "What'd he say?"

"Nothing really, he wants you to call him back. But who's Aaron?"

"Why did you answer my phone?"

He smirked and licked those sexy lips of his, "Imma go," he started to put his shoes on.

"Why?"

"Who is Aaron?" He asked again. Yep, he is jealous. Considering all the bitches he got or had. I thought about being childish and playing with him, but I don't want him to leave.

"He's my best friend," I put my phone back on the charger as I sat beside him on the bed. Gosh, he's sexy as hell. I stared at the praying hands' tattoo on his right shoulder. I've always been afraid of getting a tattoo because everybody says it hurts.

"Best friend?" He asked.

"Yes," he took his shoes back off then laid back on the bed. Aaron and I have been playing phone tag since I have been here. I haven't been able to have a full conversation with him yet. I need to tell him about these last couple of days in New Bern with Rod. This distance is new for us, but we have to maintain our friendship.

Rod flipped through the channels on the t.v. until he found something interesting to watch. He threw his arm around me, closing the gap in between us. I wrapped my leg over his and placed my arm across his stomach. He kissed my forehead, "So has this Aaron dude tried anything with you?"

"Eww, no," I said half telling the truth. Aaron has been and will always be just a friend. Our parents were best friends, so really he's more like a cousin or brother to me. I couldn't imagine doing anything with Aaron. "He's just a really good friend."

"Iight."

"What about your ex? Are you over her?"

"I've been over her, she just one of them that likes to hold on to nothing. She swears everything I do is her business."

"So, if we were to start something, will I have anything to worry about?"

"Not at all, I'm focused on you."

The next morning, still in his arms, my alarm was blaring. I turned it off, looked at the time and realized I was almost late for class. I got ready quicker than normal then went to school leaving Rod alone in my bed.

Erica and Drea were eyeing me as soon as I walked into the class. I would hate to have to curse his sister out, but I feel it's gonna happen. I sat in my desk then pulled out my materials.

"Hey!" Drea greeted me.

"Hey," I said dryly.

"How about we redeem that raincheck today after class?" Erica asked.

"Well, I have plans with your brother," I lied. I don't want to hang with her and her sidekick.

"Like what?" Drea asked.

Like none of your damn business, I thought to myself, but I responded with, "I'll know when I get home."

"He's at *your* house?" Again Drea, "I thought you weren't with him."

"Drea, shut up!" Eric told her sidekick. I'm glad she said something and not me because she was two seconds from getting her ass told off. "I'll text him to let him know you're with us. It won't take too long."

What could it hurt? I agreed to this lunch outing. When all my classes ended Erica and Drea were waiting beside my car. I followed them to the restaurant, Erica's pink mustang was cute. We ordered our Mexican food, so far so good.

"Are you and my brother an item yet?"

I laughed, these girls are so nosey. "Not yet," I answered, "but enough about me, what about y'all?"

"What do you mean?" Erica asked.

"Who are you seeing? You too Drea," now was my turn to be nosey. I gulped my root beer.

"Well, it is hard for me to date anyone, because of who my brothers are, but I do have my eye on this one guy. His name is Nick, but he has a girlfriend. We still hang out from time to time," Erica explained.

Drea said, "I'm single too. The guy I wanted found somebody else more interesting than me," I couldn't help but wonder if she were talking about Rod, it would explain all of her questions regarding our relationship.

"I hope it works out for y'all," I said more to Erica than Drea.

"We'll die old and lonely hags," Erica jokes and we all shared a laugh. We ate our food and laughed more.

"I'm having a birthday party and I like you to come. You can bring your twin too." Drea said happily.

"Cool, I love parties."

"I'm thinking of a Hawaiian theme, I'm getting flyers and invites made. It's going to be a huge deal."

"You can tell when a bitch is turning 21," Erica joked, and we laughed again.

"Whatever! Your parents did the exact same when you turned 21."

"You're 21 Erica?" I asked.

"No, I'm twenty-three. Drea is turning the same age as Chris."

"Damn, I thought you were the youngest."

"Chile, no. Quentin is twenty-nine, Rod is twenty-eight, Ray is twenty-six, I'm twenty-three, and Chris is twenty-one. Our parents didn't waste any time."

"Quentin, he's Yazzy's boyfriend and he's in jail," I said. They looked at each other before bursting out laughing.

"Quentin does not go with Yazzy's hoeing ass, and he's not in jail. He's working in Charlotte right now. Where did she come up with this shit?" Damn, why would Yazzy lie to me? What else could she be lying about? The Yazzy I know would never fix her mouth to lie to me about anything.

"Yazzy's been wanting Q for forever," Drea turned to Erica, "Do you remember when she faked a pregnancy, saying she was pregnant by him?"

"How could I forget? My mom cursed his ass out so bad, and he swore up and down he never touched her."

"Wait…" I said, "What? When?" I said in disbelief.

"Years ago. She could've got Q locked up because she was so young. I would've beaten her ass too."

"No, Yazzy was pregnant. She called me and sent a picture of the test."

"No, she wasn't," Drea shook her head.

"She called Ray to apologize for lying on Quentin. She even brought him like two pairs of shoes, and an outfit just so he'll speak to her again."

"Are you serious? If what y'all tell me is true, then Yazzy and I are gonna have a problem."

Erica pulled out her cell phone. She started to scroll on the screen before placing it to her ear. "Explain the Yazzy situation," she said into the receiver, she passed the phone to me. Quentin told me the exact story Erica and Drea just revealed to me. He added more bitches and hoes than they did, but I got the point. I became so angry I wanted to cry. I thanked Quentin for the information. I gave Erica back her phone. I gave Yazzy's bitch ass two hundred dollars for that abortion. My savings, to help a friend that was lying to me. I'm so pissed off, but I didn't show it. These bitches have kept it more real with me than my supposed friend. We finished our lunch and made plans for another day. I called Rod to see if he was still at my house, but he informed me that he went to a friend's house. He gave me the address, I really needed to talk to him.

I pulled into The Bricks, found the apartment Rod texted me. I knocked on the door, a short dark-skinned guy answered, "What's up?"

"I'm looking for Rod."

"You are?"

"LaSiah," the man was looking me up and down and I was becoming uncomfortable.

"LaSiah who?"

"JP, let her in yo," I heard Rod's deep voice. The short man stepped aside so I could enter the apartment. Rod was sitting on the couch smoking a blunt. I sat next to him. There were four other niggas in the apartment, but he didn't bother to introduce me. The apartment was foggy due to the weed smoking and it was dark as hell. The only light was from the video game Rod and one of the guys were playing.

"What's up?" He finally said to me. He was really into their football game.

"I kinda wanted to talk to you in private."

"Iight, give me a second." The smoke he blew traveled directly to my face. I sighed loudly with attitude. I wanted to walk out, but I just sat back with my arms crossed. His ass made me wait a good twenty minutes until their game was over. I was kind of amused by the shit-talking and occasionally, he'd rub my thigh. The other guys just watched them play awaiting their turn. Rod won, but he passed the controller to one of the anticipating bystanders. "I'll be back," he told them. We went up the stairs to the vacant bedroom I'm not sure which man apartment this is, but it's tidy as hell, for a guy anyway. We sat on the edge of the unmade bed. "What's going on?" He asked I'm glad I was finally getting his undivided attention.

"I had lunch with your sister and Drea," I started.

"Yeah, Erica told me. What did they start?"

I rolled my eyes at his last comment, "They told me how Yazzy faked a pregnancy."

He laughed, "That shit is ancient history yo."

"I gave her money for an abortion." I found myself getting loud with him, but my beef isn't with him it's with her lying ass.

"Damn," he said nonchalantly.

I dismissed his tone, "Quentin told me…"

"Wait, you talked to Q?"

"Yes, and he told me everything."

Rod's attitude changed completely. "Don't talk to him again yo," he said extremely calm. "I'm not fucking with him right now." I smacked my lips, this is the same nigga that claims family is everything, but he's feuding with his big brother.

I nodded, "I'm gonna confront her."

"For what? The shit with Q and Yaz is complicated, he had her all fucked up. She was in a bad space when she did that dumb shit."

"I already got the story I need, but this is more about my money and how she spent it."

"Money?" He pulled four crispy hundreds from his pockets then handed it to me. "Here's your money back and then some. You're with me, don't ever worry about money. Yaz knows she fucked up, but she doesn't need to be reminded."

"It's the principal," I said as I put the money into my wallet. I've never struggled for money, but don't lie to me about needing it. I would've done anything for that girl and all she had to do was ask. Instead, she lied and brought Quentin shit with *my* money.

"Trust me, I know. Don't sweat that shit Si." He was making light of the situation, and it didn't make me feel any better, but I know he's right. I don't need to spend any more energy stressing over two hundred dollars. After all Rod's fine ass just gave me four like it was nothing. I smiled at him.

"Thank you."

"No problem, now let's get out of here." I led us out of the room, he followed closely behind rubbing against my butt. His friends were still playing the game. "I'll holla at y'all later."

"Yeah right nigga," JP teased, "Go do your thing, come through tomorrow," I waved at the boys as we walked out the door.

Rod followed me to my house. Raymond's car was parked in my spot, I parked directly behind him, that'll teach his ass. We lay on my bed with him in between my legs. My arms rested on his chest as we watched the cooking channel. I would love for him to make the things they made because it looks so good. Raymond burst into my room with a box of pizza and two water bottles. He came just in time too because I was hungry as hell. I let him not knocking slide only because he has come bearing gifts.

"'Preciate it, bro," Rod said to him. We devoured the entire box of pizza. I was full as hell. There we were cuddling like we've known each other for years. My head nested on his chest, I listened to his heartbeat. "You smell good," he whispered. I smiled as I closed my eyes, taking in this moment. He pulled me on top of him, I straddled his lap. We gazed at one another, he cupped my face in his hands bringing me closer to him. Then it finally happened, we kissed. When our lips touched it was pure magic. His tongue was sweet like ice cream on the hottest day of summer. I felt him becoming hard through the fabric of his jeans. I smiled inside because I also was turned on by our kiss. I had a feeling this was gonna get more intense, I wanted to pull away, but I didn't. Rod's hand rubbed my ass, then he reached for the zipper on my shorts. A perfect time to stop, but I didn't. "Take these off," he broke our kiss to whisper with so much lust in his voice. I stood to step out of my shorts, just as requested. He watched my every move, I waited for what was to come next. "Lay down," he instructed. He got up to lock my bedroom door. My heart began to beat fast. He took off his shirt, tossing it on the floor. "Relax," he said as he took my white cotton panties off. I'm more nervous than a bug when it sees an exterminator. I tried to relax but to no avail. So many thoughts running through my mind, do I even want to go this far with him so soon? We've gone too far to turn back now. Rod lay right in front of my vagina, spreading my legs apart. He gently spread the folds to my vagina to lick my clit. I moaned loudly as he hungrily devoured my pussy with his mouth. I watched him as he continues to eat me out with so much precision. I threw my head back, covering my face with my hands as I came. I shivered from the intensity of the orgasm. He took my hands from my face to kiss me. I didn't even regret what just occurred. It felt good as hell. I admit Rod isn't the first guy to go down on me, but he's by far the best. We cuddled on my bed, not speaking a word. In my mind, I was replaying the wonderful moment we just shared. It could be way too soon, but I think I love him.

CHAPTER 6

Months ago, my life changed. I moved to North Carolina and I've met and fallen in love with the man of my dreams. Two things I thought would never happen happened. I'm so happy to be here with Rod, and honestly, he's the reason why I love being here.

Back in Georgia, Kennon is improving very well, he has awoken from the coma, but he still has a lot to process and surgeries to take place. Kendra, Shae and I went to see him two weeks ago when he awoke. He understands what happened with the car accident. I personally thought it was too early to tell him of the passing of our parents, but the doctors said he needed to know. He needs to be healed physically and mentally and, in their care, he can talk to a therapist if he needs to. It felt good seeing him, still in pain but smiling, nonetheless. His doctor was talking about putting a disc in his back, which will give him the ability to take rehab so he can walk again. Knowing my brother, the first thing he's gonna do when he gets out of that hospital is to go to a basketball court, and I can't wait to see him in action. According to the doctor, Kennon is going to make a full recovery. Music to my ears! We've lost enough.

I've completely stopped talking to Yazzy. She calls, but I don't answer. What type of bitch fakes a pregnancy…twice? Rod told me Chris made her ass pee on the stick in front of him, negative. Who the fuck does that? Even thinking about her gets me mad. If I'm not hanging with Rod, I go out with Drea and Erica. I can't call them friends, because I'm only with them to pass the time by until Rod calls. Classes are over for Thanksgiving break, and I'm ready to enjoy this time away starting with tonight. Drea's finally twenty-one and this fool is throwing a Luau in November. I'm excited about the party but more excited about Thanksgiving. Rod invited me to spend it with him and his family, so that means I will be meeting his parents. I'm nervous and excited at the same time, six days until the day. But lately, I don't know where Rod's head been at, I mean we've been chilling, but he still hasn't asked me or said anything about being his girlfriend. We've been doing boyfriend and girlfriend things. I performed my firsthand job a couple of days ago, by far not my favorite thing to do, but if it gets him off then I'm all for it. But since it seems like he doesn't want to step up and ask me to be with him then I'm going to enjoy my little single night.

Drea rented a building down the street from my house to host her party. I dressed in an outfit I found online, a multi-colored grass skirt with a white long-sleeved top. I completed my look with multi-colored leis. I looked at myself in the mirror, and I'm pleased with how my outfit turned out. As simple as it is, it took weeks to find something nice. Since Rod had some errands to run, I'm going to the party with Shae. She's not a fan of Drea or Erica, but a party is a party and it doesn't matter who is hosting it, we're going to have fun. "Please tell me you're ready," Shae stated when she approached the door frame. Of course, we're dressed similar, but instead of a white shirt, she opted to wear a neon green one, her favorite color.

I put on my boots to match hers. "Yep, I'm all set."

"Well let's go, I'm ready to see my man," she smiled. Raymond and Shae have made it official about a month ago. I'm so annoyed with them. He flaunts her around town letting everyone know that she's taken by him. I can admit that I am a bit jealous. I crave for Rod to flaunt me around New Bern to let everyone know that I'm his. But I'm not quite his…yet. I just hope I don't have to wait too much longer.

When Shae and I stepped into the party, it was flooded with a lot of people, and hot. Some people were dressed to the theme and others were not. I doubt if Drea cared as long as people showed up. Inside was dimly lit, but I spotted Erica almost immediately. I waved at her as I curiously looked for Drea who was shockingly not beside her. Those two are hardly ever separate.

"Ray!" Shae shrieked, breaking my concentration. She jumped into his arms and they instantly started to tongue each other down. Talk about an awkward moment. Since Raymond was already here, I searched around for Rod, but he wasn't anywhere to be found. I became irritated, not only at the fact that he wasn't here yet, but also because he hasn't even called or texted me all day. It's going to be a long night for me; I can already feel it. I excused myself from Shae and Raymond, letting her know I was going to get a desperately needed drink from the bar window. Once I retrieved my twenty-ounce cup of pineapple rum, I downed it within seconds. That should keep me two or three notches above sober.

"Heeeyyyy biiiitttccchhhh," Drea screamed into my ear. Baby girl is clearly already wasted. She started to fall all over me and shit.

"Happy Birthday!" I screamed back at her.

She grabbed my hand to lead me through the crowd of dancers, "This…my…song," she slurred. We danced together, and I started to feel the effects of my own alcohol. A couple of songs later we were sitting at the decorated tables. Drea's head was on the table and she was exhausted, but I'm just getting started. I left her at the table so I could grab myself another drink. I downed that one as well. When I found my way back to Drea she was rocking to the beats.

"Where's Erica?" I asked her, once again scanning the room.

"Probably sucking Nick's dick," we both shared a hysterical laugh.

"Hey, that rhymes…Nick, dick," we laughed even harder. My liquor has caught up with me now. I looked around one last time for Rod but still didn't see him so fuck it. "I'm going to dance," I stood. I'm drunk, but I'm good.

"Okay, I'm coming," she followed me back out. We danced with countless of guys.

Shae walked over to me with Raymond in tow. "We're gonna go, you good on a ride or do you need my car?"

"I can take her," Drea slurred. Shae looked at her like she was crazy.

"Um… no thank you, Siah call me when you're ready."

"Okay," I burped. They left the party, probably going to go fuck because that's all they do. Drea and I continue to dance, if only Shae was this fun, even Erica came to dance with us. I stopped dancing to call Rod, but he didn't answer. Drea brought me another drink, I sipped it slowly. I'm already drunk as hell.

"What's up," I heard a voice say into my ear. I turned around to a brown-skinned, medium height guy staring at me. He had one of those spongy fros I've seen these New Bern guys rock. He had his dyed a honey blonde color. His head is a major turnoff, but nevertheless, he's cute. He was dressed in Hawaiian looking joggers and a plain white T-shirt. "You're Rod's new girl, right?"

I was taken aback like I'm a part of Rod's collection or some shit. Let me find out Rod has other bitches. I wasn't even going to respond to his question. Shit, I didn't know how to respond. This guy is not my type, but with the amount of liquor I've consumed, he can pass time by. I danced with him through a couple of songs. I started to feel like I was floating in the air. So serene and carefree. Even with all these people around me, in my mind, I was completely alone. The music literally running through my veins. Drea was having the time of her life, dancing with whoever, whenever. I caught her kissing somebody at one point. This girl is too wild for me. I drifted away from her with my little friend in tow. We sat in the corner of the room attempting to make a conversation. The loud music was the blame for all the huhs and repeat that I was serving him. I couldn't hear him, and I was getting irritated by trying. He signaled for me to sit on his lap to continue the supposed conversation. I did only to be nice. He talked about himself, I don't know if he said his name was Calvin or Alvin.

"Si?" I heard loud and clear over the loud music. Of course, Rod shows up now.

My stomach dropped, I felt like I was caught up. But the liquor told me otherwise. "Hey Rod," I said to him still sitting on Calvin Alvin's lap. "I've been waiting for you."

"I see," he cut his eyes. He pulled me up and I fell all over him, "you're seriously drunk as fuck right now?"

"So?" I fixed myself. Calvin Alvin made an escape. "Damn, you scared my friend off. I was just getting to know him."

"Friend? Right," he laughed. "Let's go, I'm taking you home." He wasn't as angry or jealous as I hoped he'd be.

"Where were you all night?" I asked him once we were in his car. He didn't say anything as we headed towards my house. I asked the same question again, but this time a little louder, maybe he didn't hear me the first time. I was feeling the headache that I know will hit harder in the morning. He pulled in front of my house, letting the engine run. "Are you going to walk me in?" I asked.

He sighed heavily, "Yeah," he said while turning the car off. I flopped on my bed as soon as I entered my room. The crisp cold sheets clung to my body. He stood at the door for a minute. I took off the leis and hula skirt, that was starting to itch, tossing them at the foot of my bed. "Iight, yo," he started to leave.

"No!" I sat up, "I want to know where you've been tonight?"

"I've been handling business," he sat next to me on the bed.

I wrapped my arms around his broad shoulders, "I was waiting for you."

He chuckled, "Waiting for me while with another nigga?" He raised his voice. I knew he was jealous of my encounter with Calvin Alvin.

"We were just having a conversation," I sat back against the pillows. "Besides, I'm not your girl," I mumbled.

"Right, and you will never be acting like that."

Oh, I was pissed. Up until the party I've been doing everything to show him that I want to be his girlfriend. I'm tired, and I know other niggas are interested in me and without hesitation will make me theirs. "Get out!" I yelled. Emotions taking over me. I could've been by his side all night, but his lame-ass business stood in the way of that.

"No, we're adults, let's talk," he looked me in the eyes.

"No, get the fuck out my house."

He chuckled again, "You wanted me here, so here I am. I'm not going anywhere." He smiled and it annoyed me. The nerve of this nigga. I stood staring at him with my arms folded. I wanted him gone and I want him gone now, but he didn't play me no mind. He laid back in the spot I occupied and lit a blunt. I wanted to knock the shit from his mouth, but Daddy always told me to never put my hands on a man unless it was to defend myself. I could spit fire at this point. He knows I want to be with him, and I want it a little too badly. I will not allow this man to string me along. I've lost, I always lose, but that's okay. Now I know where I stand with him, why did I have to fall so fast? I marched to my bathroom to shower, maybe this water will wake me up, clear my emotions. I wanted to cry so bad, but I won't. He was still lying in the same spot when I returned, I laid beside him without speaking a word. I was hurt, but I didn't want to show that to him. Rod suddenly leaned over to kiss me, I wanted to pull away, but I accepted his lips and tongue. I could taste the liquor from his tongue. I kiss him deeply; his left hand made its way inside my panties. I moaned as I placed my hand over his as he fingered me. His fingers brought warmth to my tender spot. A perfect fit. His fingers danced in my wetness, sliding in and out, making small circles on my clitoris. I suckled on his neck as I muffled moans. "Look at me," he said. I felt sheepish from the way he was watching me. He continued to play in my vagina as he watched me, I moaned to his every touch. I could hear the squishy sounds coming from my valley in the quiet room. I came…hard. He held his glistening fingers to my lips, he enjoyed the view as I licked his fingers. I tasted myself. Rod lifted my tank top exposing my bare breasts, without hesitation he cupped them lifting each one to his eager mouth. It felt so good and I was becoming even wetter. I've never felt like this before. My hands were all over his body. Amid him giving my breast his undivided attention, I unbuckled his pants. Our eyes met again as I freed his hard penis. I grabbed it firmly but gently with my soft hands. He moaned as I massaged it, closing his eyes as he melted at my touch. I love the faces he makes as I lead him on the road to his own climax. I like pleasuring him and I love the way he pleasures me. An hour ago, I was telling this man to leave my house, and he would've possibly been out my life, but now I don't want him to ever go anywhere. Rod positioned himself between my legs, sliding my panties off. He looked up smiling at me. I sat up just a little to pull his shirt off then I tossed it in the corner. I kissed his chest. "Lie back," he instructed in a whisper. He dove right into my valley. Licking every hill and making his way to my river. I moaned his name, he watched me as he dined on me. He was licking me so carefully and with so much passion almost like I was the best meal he'd ever tasted. The most delectable treat to grace his tongue. I came again but harder this time. We shared a long kiss. "Can I put the tip in?" he whispered into my ear.

I shook my head, I don't think I'm fully ready for that yet. "No," I moaned.

Rod kissed my neck and I melted, "Please baby," he kissed me again. He slowly entered me, and I immediately tensed up. I closed my eyes tightly, "Relax," he whispered in my ear. I tried, but I couldn't. I've never gone this far before, inch by inch he slid inside of me, I gasped from the pressure. It hurt like hell, but not as I imagined. He worked his hips sliding in slowly and out even slower. I feel like I'm dreaming, but I don't want to wake up. Rod's sweet sweat dripping onto my face. I wrapped my legs around him. We moaned from passion. I let all my thoughts leave my mind and went with the flow. He kissed me the entire time. I held onto his waist, I moaned loudly. My body was doing things it had never done before, feeling things it hadn't felt before. "Damn, you feel so good," Rod grunted increasing his pace. I gripped the sheets as I neared yet another climax. He went deeper in me as I moaned his name, "Ahh," he moaned he filled me with his cum. This is a magical moment and experience that I never want to forget. He collapsed beside me, and I rested my head on his chest. Rod held me tightly. The light from the morning started to grace my bedroom's window. "How do you feel?"

I smiled, "I feel good," I rubbed his stomach. "I love you," I blurted. I cursed myself as soon as the words escaped my lips. I should've waited until he said it first, but I mean it. I feel it so that's not so wrong. I love Rod, and I honestly think I've loved him since the first day we met. I can't hide how I feel about him, so I'm happy I did say it.

He lifted my chin to gaze into my eyes, "I love you too, Si."

I smiled so hard inside. I'm one happy girl. "After that," I said referring to our sex session of him taking my virginity. "Where does that leave us?"

"You've always been mine, titles don't define me, but if you need it said then I'll say it. Do you want to be my girl?"

I smiled, "I want to be your girl," we shared a kiss, our first kiss as a couple. Now I can keep calm about Thanksgiving dinner. We made love again.

We woke up at a quarter to eight, "I'll be back," Rod said to me quietly. He was fully dressed. He kissed me goodbye. I stretched when he left out my door. I can't believe I had sex! I had sex! Wow! Although it didn't go like I've planned in my head. I had so many expectations. I wanted music…no music. I wanted a glow in the dark condom…no condom at all. I guess things are better unplanned. I jumped up to shower and pee. I didn't want to wash his scent from my body, but I needed to shower. I had a little blood on the tissue when I used the bathroom. I wanted to freak out, but I smiled knowing he popped my cherry! I put on my long-sleeved, flannel pajama set, then went downstairs to make a bowl of my favorite cinnamon cereal. Today is my chill day. I cleaned up my room, put our clothes in my hamper, then started to catch up on my shows. I texted Drea to make sure she got home okay. She did and we agreed to have lunch tomorrow. Shae barged into my room just as I was completing one episode, she was also in pajamas. Great minds.

"What's up?" She said, sitting on the floor.

"Hey," I paused the show.

"What happened last night?" She asked. "Ray said Rod had to drag you home."

"Um…first of all, he didn't drag me anywhere. I just had a little too much to drink."

"Why?" She had a concerned look on her face.

"Because I wanted to have a good time," why is this bitch questioning me? I'm grown.

"Are you feeling some type of way right now? Cause of Mommy and Daddy?"

I immediately became irritated. What the fuck does she mean? I will always feel some type of way about not having my parents here with me. "Shae, it's not a problem, trust me. All for fun," I rolled my eyes.

"I'm only asking." The tension in the room was thick. She never wanted to talk about Mom and Dad before so don't start now. I've had more conversations and venting sessions with Sam than I've had with Shae. I miss my parents so much, but I will not drown my sorrows with a bottle of liquor. Mom and Dad are not coming back, I've come to terms with that. I'm on cloud nine right now and I don't want to come down. "Anyway," Shae said, changing the subject. "You fucked Rod?"

I looked at her sideways. Did he tell Raymond? Did Raymond turn around and tell her? It's only been hours ago and somebody other than the two of us knows. "What?" I questioned. I'm not comfortable with him telling anyone. I think he should have asked me first before he started telling people. "What makes you ask that?"

She knocked on the wall, "These walls are paper thin Siah. We heard y'all doing something last night. So, have y'all had sex?"

I nodded, "Yes we did" I grinned. A recap of our love making flashed in my head.

"Bitch!" She jumped on me happily. I pushed her off playfully. "How was it? Your ass wasn't even going to tell me."

"I was going to tell you. It was good too," I said shyly.

"I can't believe you're not a virgin anymore! Are y'all finally a couple too? Because he's not about to have sex with you and ya'll still be friends" I nodded again. "About time, because I was about to approach him on some real shit." She laughed, Shae is crazy, and I have no doubt that she would have said something to him. "Welcome to the Hill family!" She smiled.

"Shut up," I smiled as well. We talked for hours, just catching up on stuff we didn't even know we missed out on. I could tell something was bothering her, but she didn't speak on it. If the issue is too big then she'll come to me about it.

As soon as Shae left my phone started to ring. I looked at the caller id: Aaron. I rolled my eyes because he hasn't called me in months. I'm not a good friend either because I haven't called him either. I've been so focused on Rod and getting to know him that I kind of forgot all about Aaron.

"Well hey boo!" I said into the receiver. Aaron and I always called each other boo.

"Hey Siah," it wasn't Aaron's voice on the other end of the phone, but it was a voice that was familiar to me, Olivia, an insecure bitch that I never cared for. Why is she calling me? And why from Aaron's phone? "It's Olivia," she said.

"Hey, what's up?" I asked trying to sound cheery. Aaron will most definitely hear my mouth about this little phone call.

"I'm calling to find out if you and Aaron are still together."

I laughed, "Are you serious?"

"Yes," she sounded desperate, "We're together now but…"

"What are you doing?" I heard Aaron's voice. "Hello?" he said after a couple of seconds of muffles.

"Aaron," I said sternly. He knows how much I hate to be contacted by his chick of the week.

"Siah, I'm sorry. This girl is crazy."

"So, you and Olivia?"

He sighed, "Something like that, how you been stranger?"

"Very good, up until that phone call. No bitch should call my shit from your line, period." I tore into him.

"I know Siah and…"

"On some dumb shit too bro," I cut him off. "Asking me if we're together then in the same breath say that y'all are now, what kind of shit is that? Aaron, you need to reassure her that there is nothing was nothing and will never be anything between us."

"Why do you have her name tatted on you, Aaron?" I could hear Olivia in the background ask him.

I snickered, "Yeah Aaron," I mocked her. Now, this is pure entertainment. Aaron and I were drunk one night and decided to go to one of his cousin's houses. His cousin was having a tattoo party. Mix tattoo and liquor and bad things happen. Long story short, Aaron thought he was getting a tattoo of his mother's name, but I convinced the guy to put my name. He was livid, but we worked it out so that he forgave me.

"Shut up," he said playfully.

"I don't know why I even try with you," Olivia shouted.

"Bye then, you're bitching for no reason."

"Aaron, call me back later," I said to him.

"No, she's the one with the problem, plus we need to catch up." I love my best friend. He needs to keep his hoes in check, but I like how he doesn't put anybody before me.

"You've been ducking me," I joked.

"Naw, just working like crazy. I finally got my own apartment."

"Wow! Congratulations. Now I have somewhere to stay when I come to town."

"Of course, speaking of...when are you coming for a visit?"

"I'm still trying to learn the ins and outs of this town, but I do want to visit very soon. You can always come here for a visit too."

"I'll do that," Aaron and I talked for a while. It felt good hearing his voice, that country Effingham accent that I've missed so much. Rod walked in and I knew it was time to end my conversation with Aaron.

I smiled at Rod as I was saying my goodbyes to my friend. He kissed my forehead. He smells so good, "Hey," I said, setting my phone aside. He sat at the edge of my bed and wrapped himself in my giraffe printed fleece.

"What's up, baby? It's cold as fuck." He kicked off his shoes, "Come warm me up." I straddled his waist and hugged him tightly, he draped the cover around us with his cold hands resting on my warm lower back. When I'm with Rod, nothing and nobody matter. Just us against the world.

"I'm hungry," I said nibbling on his ear.

"You're always hungry, yo." I sat up to look into his eyes, "What do you want to eat?"

"Anything."

"Anything, huh?" He said slyly.

"Not like that," I pushed him playfully. "I want to go somewhere."

"Get dressed."

We went to eat lunch at a Jamaican spot in Havelock. Talk about some banging ass food, the restaurant was culturally decorated. Easy on the eyes, the staff was amazing, I felt like I was their long-lost Jamaican cousin or something. I was more than stuffed once I finished my meal, I had to unbuckle my pants. To and from Havelock we held hand in the car. We went back to his house, I noticed unfamiliar cars in the driveway. With a confused look on my face, I asked, "Are your parents' home?"

"Yeah," he smirked.

I quickly buckled my pants. He could've told me we were coming back to his place so I could meet his parents, I would've gotten cuter. "Rod!" I punched him in the arm.

"Baby calm down. They wanted to meet you before Thursday. Since Ray brought your sister over, I thought you'll feel more comfortable."

I got jealous once he mentioned Shae being here. This is supposed to be my moment. Shae and I have shared everything, and I didn't want to share meeting my man's parents with her too. I took a deep breath, "Okay let's do this."

Raymond was walking out when we were approaching the door. He informed us that he was going to smoke, but Rod asked him to wait on him. He sulked, but he came back inside with us. When we went into the living room, I turned on my best smile. Shae was sitting next to the boys' mother looking through photo albums.

"Hey," I said waving. Why did I wave? They noticed me at the same time.

"Hey! Come join us," Rod's mom said. I sat on the vacant side of the couch next to her. "This is Rod when he was six months old." She pointed to a picture of little Rod in a little blue jumpsuit.

I snickered, "You were so cute," I told Rod. He nodded, he's so full of himself. Rod and Raymond went towards the back of the house, leaving Shae and me alone with their mother. I couldn't even get a formal introduction like Mom this is…..and Si this is. Just threw me to the wolves, but from what I can tell she seems nice.

"Ray informed me that you're Chasity's girls"

"Yes ma'am," we responded in unison. She got up to retrieve another photo album from the bookcase. I noticed how small her frame was. She wore a long, curly weave that looked like she spent a fortune on it. She wore an African smock that stopped just below her knees. Indeed, a cute lady. She joined us back on the couch, then opened the album. On the first page was a picture of our mother and her. This picture was at least twenty years old. I could've cried as I looked at the picture of my mother, so full of life.

"Chasity was my best friend from grade school all the way up to high school," She spoke, "We were inseparable," she chuckled. I didn't know Mom had friends. In Georgia, her life revolved around her family and work. Mostly work. Mom's occupation of a prison guard required long days and even longer nights, but she loved her job. She changed some of the prisoners' lives. At the funeral, a couple of them wrote cards expressing how much she meant to them and what she did for them. Mom was extremely optimistic, that's something I get from her. "I'm sorry girls, I didn't mean," Rod's mom apologized. I'm guessing she thought she may have offended us since Shae, and I became silent.

"No, it's okay," Shae reassured her. "It's actually nice to see that our mother had a social life."

I nodded in agreement, "Yes our mom never talked about her life in New Bern," I added.

"Well, we did grow apart when we got into relationships and started having babies. Chasity called me to tell me she and Vince decided to move to Georgia, and I was happy for her. Hell, I wanted to go with her. We'd call or text each other to wish each other a happy birthday every year and to check on the children, but that's about it. I loved your mom and I'm deeply sorry for the loss you and your family had to endear." She stared off into space as she spoke. I'm so glad Rod, Raymond, and an older man, who I presumed was the dad, walked back into the living room because I was on the verge of tears. I miss my mom so much and it's the little things that get to me. I looked at Rod with my glossy eyes, he had a look of concern. I tried not to blink because if I did the tears, I was praying so hard not to fall would have fallen.

"Robin, enough of the albums for one day. I'm sure…" he paused making a gesture at me and Shae.

"LaShae," she stood to shake his hand.

I did the same, "LaSiah."

He continued, "LaShae and LaSiah have had enough traveling down memory lane."

She smiled as she closed the album. He returned it to the shelf. Rod came over to me, "What's wrong?" He whispered into my ear. I shook my head. For the remainder of the evening, Shae and I put on our best faces and behavior for their parents. We talked about our goals in life and they even encouraged us to pursue our dreams. They're cool in my book, and I'm glad to have experienced this moment with my twin. Mr. Quentin Sr. and Mrs. Robin said we were welcomed at their home any time as we sipped on a hot cup of chamomile tea.

"Can you girls stay for dinner?" Mr. Quentin asked.

"Yes, we would love to," Shae answered for us.

"Great! Any allergies?" We both shook our heads. We love food and we'd eat anything placed in front of us. Remember, our father was frugal, and he didn't play that picky eating shit. "The food will be done soon, we'll call you down," He walked away with Mrs. Robin in tow. The four of us looked at each other contemplating our next move.

"Shae and I are going to the den," Raymond said.

"Tight, we're going into the hot tub," Rod said.

"Oh, I want to go in the hot tub too," Shae protested Raymond.

Raymond shook his head, "Naw. See you in a minute, Bro."

Rod smiled at me. It's cold as fuck outside and he wants to get in a hot tub. I'm just going with the flow. He led me through the kitchen past his parents to a small room with a white jacuzzi in the center of it. Attached to the jacuzzi was a small tv screen. It's starting to seem like the Hill Family may be a bit materialistic. I mean my parents would never spend money on stuff like this. We had a trampoline and an in-ground pool in our back yard and that's it. I'm not complaining or judging them by no means, after all, it is their money and they can do as they please. I looked around the room from the black tiled flooring to the only window. The walls were black, and the lighting is very dim. Imagine a room with all black and the only colors come from the jacuzzi, and the water. The room was very warm and was getting warmer with every step we took toward the jacuzzi. I noticed an 'H' engraved in the bottom of the tub, the clear blue water was still until Rod turned on the jet stream.

"Come on," he said. He took his shirt off, his abs glistened in the darkroom.

"I don't have a bathing suit," I said stating the obvious.

"Take all your clothes off," he removed the rest of his clothes then entered the tub.

"No! Somebody might come in."

"Nobody comes in here Si," he got out the tub, came close behind me. He grabbed my waist then kissed my neck, "Please," he whispered. I was reluctant, but I thought, 'Why not?' If anybody comes in here, I'm killing Rod's ass. I took off my clothes then we got into the warm, bubbling tub. It's like I walked into heaven. We splashed each other before collapsing into each other's arms. I draped my arms around his neck, he rested his hands on my ass, rubbing and grabbing handfuls under the water. He was turning me on, right in his parents' house with them being steps away. I bit on my bottom lip. I would've never imagined myself being in a jacuzzi naked, especially with a naked guy. "What happened earlier?" He asked.

I shook my head, "Nothing, I just didn't know your mom knew mine."

"My mom knows everybody," he chuckled.

"It made me a bit emotional seeing her picture. My mom didn't share her past with us."

"Maybe she didn't want to dwell in the past. I can understand that. She wanted to build with her family," I nodded. Rod has a point. I drew in closer to him to kiss his juicy lips, I kissed him deeply, I want to focus on him. He continued to grip my ass as he backed me into the corner of the tub. My hands running up and down his back. He picked me up and I wrapped my legs around his waist. He tenderly kissed my neck. He gave me the same seductive look he gave me last night. He was horny and so was I. I've been craving for him to be inside me again. Last night when he filled me with his penis was the most, I'd ever felt complete, and it wasn't only the sex, it's the connection we have. He slowly stroked his penis under the water then slid in me. I moaned loudly, it echoed off the wall. "Ssshh baby," he moaned in my ear. We made love in the tub and we tried our best to stay quiet, but as we neared our climax, we let go. I didn't care if the whole world could hear our lovemaking. Once we were finished, we cleaned up the room and put our clothes on our semi damp bodies. Rod not only makes love to my body, but also to my soul. We managed to make it to his room unseen. He closed the door putting a towel down to cover the threshold. He grabbed his pack of blunts and the weed from his closet. He sat at the foot of the bed to roll up, he smoked to reach his happy space. I sat back watching him, I'm such a creep when it comes to him, but I love looking at him. I love how he's all mine, my first real boyfriend and my first lover. I am so lucky to have him and can't imagine being with another man. No matter how much Rod makes me mad, I'm his forever, and he's mine forever. We were called to the dinner table shortly after he finished his blunt. His parents prepared bacon-wrapped chicken, mashed potatoes with gravy, corn on the cob, and yeast rolls. We drunk a bottle of wine with our dinner. They shared stories about the boys and all the trouble they used to get into. I could tell family dinner is a must in their home. Everybody was at the table and it didn't seem forced.

Rod and I went to his room where we made love all night. We were exploring every aspect of each other's body. He said I was the first girl he'd ever gone down on. I find that awfully hard to believe, his skills are up there, he makes me come multiple times from his tongue alone.

His phone woke me at six a.m. I reached over his sleeping body to retrieve it. I figured it was his alarm, and it needed to shut up.

I rubbed my eyes and noticed he was getting a phone call. With a scrunched face I wondered who the fuck could be calling him at this hour. The number wasn't saved, so I did what any black woman in my shoes would have done. I answered the call.

I didn't have to say anything before the person on the other end started bumping their gums, "Rod! Rod! Are you with her because we have to talk?" The person said. Clearly, she was drunk.

Now, this very moment I had two options: hang up or play it all the way through. I chose the latter because I want to know who this chick is. This unsaved number chick. My heart felt like it was pounding so loud, I was afraid it'll wake him. I have to tell myself this situation is just like when bitches called me for Aaron.

I put on my best impression of Rod, "Yo," I said in a deep voice, one that I felt resembled his.

"I might be pregnant."

"Pregnant?!" I said in my voice, it came out louder than expected. Rod jumped up trying to grab the phone. I moved away from him, "Who is this?" I said sternly. Rod stood in front of me holding his hand out for his phone.

"Ask your *man* who I am," she said viciously before hanging up. I looked at the phone in disbelief. I can't believe what just transpired. I must be dreaming.

I handed Rod his phone, "Who was that?" I asked.

He looked at his phone with a confused look. "I don't know," he stared at the number like he had no idea who was calling *his* phone.

I just gave this nigga all of me and this shit happens. Why couldn't this have happened before I gave him my virginity? "Well, the bitch that you don't know thinks she's pregnant by you," I yelled at him.

"Si, calm down, it's some mad bitch prank calling my phone, that shit isn't real, you tight for no reason," he came closer to me, taking my hand.

"Who plays like that?"

He led me back to his bed. "New Bern bitches," he chuckled. Rod and I made love, thoughts of him being with another chick escaped my mind. There is no way anybody else is occupying his time.

I daydreamed as Rod snored lightly next to me. Have you ever stopped to admire your significant other's body? Like really pay close attention to every nook and cranny? I always take in parts of Rod's body, I probably know it better than he does. Rod's beard is thick and jet black. It really compliments his chocolate skin tone. It hugs his face so well and I love the way it feels when he's down there letting my juices flow on it. For a guy that doesn't spend a single second in the gym he has extremely broad, muscular cut shoulders with wash board abs. My pink colored fingernails run across those abs every night. Let's take a moment to focus on that monster that he possesses between his thighs. It has a crook in it, not much, but I can tell. The girth of that thing is out of this world. I can hardly wrap my hands around it when I'm jacking him off. It nudges through his pants when we are extremely close. One time when he was asleep, and I stared at his penis. It's fascinating how it's slightly darker than his complexion, but the tip of it is lighter. The plumpness of the mushroom shaped head is what I love to focus on the most. I love how it feel when I run my fingertips across it. But that's the physical aspects of Rod, I've noticed that when something is bothering him, he smokes to clear his mind. He will sit for hours in his own thoughts. I've started to massage his back when this happens, this relaxes him as well. I enjoy making him happy.

CHAPTER 7

It's finally Thanksgiving Day and I'm helping Mrs. Robin prepare the side dishes. Shae and Raymond are working on the desserts. Rod and Mr. Quentin are outside frying two turkeys. Chris and his girlfriend, Emory, are setting the table. Erica is washing the dishes that we used already. All hands were definitely on deck. Erica told me she invited Nick, but he had other engagements with his girlfriend. She was in her room pouting until Mr. Quentin made her come wash the dishes. Let's be real, she knows the man has a girlfriend so what does she expect from him? That's the problem with some of these females, they are so comfortable with being the side chick. I refuse. If it weren't for Mrs. Robin I wouldn't be here today. Rod still has a lot of explaining to do. He thought fucking me back to sleep that night made me forget what occurred, but he's dead wrong. I want answers and I want them sooner rather than later. He danced around the whole issue all week, but he's been trying to be extra romantic. He had my favorite flowers delivered to my house, but even the lilies won't save him from my wrath. He's been making me breakfast in bed all week, but all the gestures only make me believe he's guilty. I've had his phone all week and the unsaved number hasn't called, but I shouldn't have to monitor my boyfriend's phone. That's a sign of insecurity and I'm not insecure, but I better not find out anything or it's a wrap for us.

"Be careful honey," I heard Mrs. Robin say. I was so caught up in my own thoughts I forgot I was cutting collard greens, I almost nicked my finger. I have way too much on my mind. I want it all cleared soon. I rushed through the rest of the preparations before I went to lay down in Rod's room. I have a major headache.

A call came through on my phone and it scared me, I wasn't expecting any calls today, without looking at the caller id I answered, "Hello?" I said. I looked at Rod's spiral painted ceiling.

"Hey Siah," the voice said faintly, but I think I know this voice.

"Kennon?" I questioned, I haven't talked to him on the phone since the accident and his voice sounds so different.

"Yeah," he cleared his throat, "Happy Thanksgiving."

"Happy Thanksgiving," I was so happy to hear him say that. He was barely speaking the last time we visited him.

"What are y'all doing today?"

"Shae and I are at our boyfriend's house, we're having dinner with them and Kendra is with Peanut at the house. What about you?"

"Sam brought me a plate of what she cooked. So, you know I can come home next week, right?"

"Yes, Sam told me. I'll be there to get you," I said happily. Shae and I already made the arrangements to drive her car to Georgia to pick him up.

"Alright, just making sure. I'm ready to get out of this hospital." I know he's tired of being in there, it has been almost two years. I'm just so thankful the doctors did not give up on him. When the accident first occurred, Kennon didn't show any signs of brain functions, they though he was brain dead. But with powerful praying that test proved to be a lie. They monitored him closely and found out there was a glitch. He had brain functions, but the swelling concerned them. Shae and I agreed to them putting him in a coma. What was supposed to be weeks of the coma took a month, but his survival was all that mattered. He gave me a list of games he wanted us to bring for him. Typical Little Brother. We all put together his room months ago, so he should feel right at home when he gets here.

Rod entered the room as I was hanging up with Kennon. He opened the shades, letting in the sunlight from outside. "What's wrong?" he asked me. I told him of my headache, he came to hug me, but I tensed up. He noticed, he looked at me and all I could do was hang my head. I didn't mean to get tensed it just happened. "What else is bothering you?" he asked.

I shook my head, "Its nothing, I'm just waiting on dinner." How can I trust him? I'm putting up a wall until I find out the truth about the situation. Something in me is telling me not to believe him.

"Cool," he said before leaving his room. I expected him to investigate more, but whatever. I sat there in my own thoughts. A buzz broke my trance. I checked my phone, no notification. I looked around, I spotted Rod's phone on the floor, it must have fallen from his pocket. I got up to grab it, and he had a text message from Yazzy telling him Happy Thanksgiving. I rolled my eyes as I deleted it. I held my breath as I scrolled through the recent call log, but nothing alarming. Thank God. Rod is really redeeming himself. I smiled inside, but I had one last thing to check. I memorized the number from the other night, I dialed it from his phone then hit send. Hoping for…damn I'm not sure what I'm hoping for.

"Hello?" the unsaved number girl questioned with excitement in her voice. My blood started to boil instantly.

"Bitch…" I paused because I wanted her to feel the rage behind the word. "I'm only going to ask you this one fucking time. Who the fuck are you?" I asked through clenched teeth.

"Um…I'm…I'm…" she stammered. I wish I could've reached into the phone to slap the shit out of her.

"Spit it out," I yelled into the phone. I kept my eyes on Rod who was back outside with his father.

"I don't want to cause any problems," she stated, but if she doesn't tell me who the hell she is, it will be hell to pay. She sounded so afraid which only stirred up a side of me that I didn't know was there over a nigga. Rod is mine until I have proof that he's being untrue to me. I didn't say anything, I was tired of the hesitation. I needed her lame-ass to answer the question before Rod returns. "Rod is going to kill me," I heard her mumble under her breath. After what felt like a couple of minutes pass by, she finally answered, "My name is Teana," she sighed.

"His ex?" I questioned.

"Yeah, if you say so."

"Do you know who I am?"

"He told me that y'all are talking, but it's nothing serious."

I didn't respond to the 'he said' shit. "Are y'all still messing around?"

"Most definitely."

"Me and Rod are together," I said matter-of-factly, but it seemed like saying that was a lost cause. "Last week you said something about a pregnancy?" Rod was still in the back yard sitting on the lawn furniture.

"I said I think I am, but Rod knows this. I apologize for being rude because my problem isn't with you. He was ignoring my calls all day and I was fed up."

"How far along?"

"I don't know, maybe six weeks."

"Six weeks? Like two months pregnant?" I wanted to break down because he's been messing with the both of us. Granted we've just had sex, but we were doing other sexual things. Now to find out he's been doing sexual things with this chick is a slap in the face.

"Yes, I'm sorry," she kept apologizing and for what? She didn't do me wrong, he did. "I'm not messy or anything. I want him to be there like he said he'd be."

"I'm sure he will be but look I gotta go. Nice talking to you and good luck with everything."

"Wait, please don't tell him you talked to me." I hung up right in her ear. I'm not concerned about her, fuck her. My whole problem is my supposed boyfriend. This shit right here is too much for one person to handle. I packed up the items I had around the room. I contemplated for a second. I don't want to start a scene at his parent's house on this holiday, but I don't want to eat with his cheating and lying ass either. I curse myself for falling too deep and giving him so much of me without knowing every inch of him. Silly me. Emory knocked on the door informing me that it was dinner time. I put his phone back on the floor before leaving the room. Rod greeted me with a smile and all I could do is roll my eyes at him. I sat beside him, but I didn't say two words to him. I played nice throughout dinner. We talked about what we were thankful for and about shopping tomorrow. The food was delicious, but it had nothing on the meal my family would've prepared. The only family we had in Georgia was my dad's brother, Uncle Vernon, and boy could Uncle Vernon fry the best-fried turkey anybody could ask for. He too has passed, and I miss him so much.

I was so stuffed, but dessert was next and no matter what, I was getting some sweet potato pie. As I was making my way to the dessert table the front door flung open. A tall dark-skinned guy walked in. Spitting image of Mr. Quentin, he wore a burgundy peacoat and black slacks with burgundy moccasins. Dude had style and fine as hell. This has to be Quentin he confirmed my thought when he spoke, "What's up?" I remembered his voice from the phone call awhile back.

"Hi," I said awestruck.

"Don't tell me y'all are finished eating," he closed the door slowly and quietly.

"Kinda, I mean we're eating dessert now." I pointed toward the dessert table filled with all types of cakes, pies, and tarts.

"Damn, Dad's gonna chew my ass out. I tried to get here sooner but…" He sighed "I'm Q," he extended his hand out.

"I know…LaSiah," I shook his soft hand.

"Tyrrod's girl, right?" I rolled my eyes, "Damn, what Little Bro do?" he chuckled.

"I'm going to get pie," I said walking off.

"I'm coming too," he followed. I cut a piece of pecan and sweet potato pie. He fixed a plate of macaroni and cheese, rice and fish. Fish I didn't see at the dinner table. He saw me eyeing his plate, "I'm pescatarian, Ma makes sure I'm accommodated."

I laughed, "So you're spoiled?"

He chuckled, "Yeah, I like being spoiled too. Don't you like being spoiled?" He put mustard and hot sauce on his fish. This simple task makes us instant friends even if he doesn't want to be friends. My people in Georgia love some mustard and hot sauce on their fish.

"I'm not spoiled," I answered him.

He took a huge bite of the fish. "Rod's not doing something right then," he said when he finished chewing.

I laughed, "I don't like you already."

"What?! Everybody loves Q!" He followed me back to the dining room. Everyone but Rod jumped up when they saw Q. Rod eyed me, but I didn't pay his ass any mind. I ate my slices of pies in silence. Q hugged everyone even Shae. Mr. Quentin stood to let Q take his seat.

"You should've come earlier son," Mr. Quentin said sternly.

"Sorry Pops, I was handling business. I was just telling Siah that in the back."

"Why the fuck was you talking to my girl?" Rod spoke. I wanted to be invisible when he said that. I do not need any heat on me right now.

"Tyrrod, watch your language," Mr. Quentin shot Rod a look.

Q smirked, "Little Bro act like I can't talk to his girl. Am I supposed to ignore her?"

"Yeah nigga, don't say shit to her," Rod was hot, but I couldn't understand why?

Q finished the food in his mouth, "You're protective over this one, huh? That's cool. Damn Siah seems like we can't be friends after all."

Rod slammed his fists on the table, "What the fuck did I just say, nigga?" I shot Shae our 'about to go' look. Rod now stood over Q, who was cool as a cucumber. He didn't seem threatened by Rod at all. I looked around the table at his family, Erica looked scared as hell, Chris and Raymond were just looking, and Mrs. Robin looked disappointed. This is beyond embarrassing. Mr. Quentin pulled Rod away from Q. Mrs. Robin tried to diffuse the situation by telling each of them to calm down. Q looked at me and all I could do was shake my head. I literally just met the man.

"Y'all chill man, this ain't the time," Raymond finally spoke up.

"I'm cool bro, but if this little nigga step to me again it's definitely going to be a problem. I'm trying to spare him an embarrassment in front of *his* girl." Q said calmly.

Rod still flared up, "Embarrass me, pussy ass nigga." Q stood up so fast the chair he previously occupied fell over. I got up as well because I've had enough. I pushed Rod towards the steps leading him upstairs to his room.

"I'm tired of that nigga thinking he can disrespect me. Regardless of what went down, I'm still *his* brother," I heard Q shout.

"Fuck you," Rod yelled, I continued to push him up the steps until we reached his room. I closed the door locking it behind us. "I hate his ass yo and they are treating this slime ass nigga like a king," he sat on his bed.

"Calm down," I suggested. I leaned against his door thinking about the delicious pies I just abandoned.

"Naw, fuck that and you chopping it up with the nigga after I told you not to talk to his ass," he spat.

"First of all, I'm not rude and that's your brother. If someone talks to me then I'm going to talk back."

"Well fuck you too then," he said viciously. I was taken aback. Fuck me? He's the one who has issues with his big brother probably over nothing, but it's fuck me? I grabbed the stuff I packed up to leave, but before I could turn the knob, he was pressing himself against me. "I'm sorry Baby, I didn't mean that," he apologized. I could feel his heart beating fast.

"Don't say shit like that to me," I turned to face him, and we shared a kiss. A kiss that almost made me forget what I needed to confront him about. I wrapped my arms around his neck, gazing into his light brown eyes. Eyes that used to display so much truth, but now clouded with lies. "I talked to Teana," I blurted. The look on his face was priceless. He looked disappointed.

"Who?" He questioned.

"Teana, your ex, your baby's mother. You know the bitch you're still fucking behind my back," I said calmly. He stepped back breaking our embrace.

"I don't..."

"She said all she wants from you is to be there for your child." I cut him off, "And honestly I can't agree more. Every child deserves to have their father in their life."

"Si…"

"She's six weeks by the way, but something tells me you already knew that. That pretty much means you cheated on me with her." I didn't raise my voice at him or get mad cause at the end of the day he's caught. "So, she can have you. We are done, don't call or text my phone anymore."

"Can I talk?" He asked, stepping into my personal bubble. "One, I don't have a baby on the way. Two, I've never cheated on you." He grabbed me by the waist bringing me even closer. If he thinks sexing me is going to work this time, he is sadly mistaken. "Three, I think it's fucked up how you're quick to believe a random bitch, letting her come between us. When do I have time to fuck around Si? Like for real, I'm with you every single day, all day. We're not done."

I searched his face to see if I could tell if he was lying, and I believe him. I mean we are together unless I'm at school. I'm so confused. I stared at him blankly. I pulled away from him to retrieve his phone from where I left it. I dialed the number then put it on speaker.

"Hello?" Teana answered.

"Me again, so Rod says he doesn't fuck with you," I informed her.

"He's lying. I got pictures of us and I can send you our messages," she said.

"Okay, cool. Send all of it," I began to give her my number, but before I could get the fourth digit out my mouth Rod blanked.

He took the phone from me, "Bitch, why are you lying?"

"I'm lying Rod? Really, really? You're full of shit, just be honest with that damn girl."

"You're trying to make something out of nothing, it's pathetic."

"So, you weren't just at my house the other night? Asking me for some head?"

This nigga is downright disrespectful. What have I gotten myself into? I should've walked out right then, but my dumb ass stayed there listening to them arguing back and forth about who was wrong and who was right. He's saying he never messed with her, but she's saying he did. Maybe I handled this situation all wrong. I waited until the two of them stopped bickering. I snatched the phone from him to finish giving her my number. I'll let the pictures and messages do the talking. All I need is proof.

"Si, I never fucked with her while we've been together. You have to believe that," he took my hands into his.

Confused I said, "I thought you never fucked with her at all," how can he do me like this?

"A long time ago, but that bitch is fraud yo." I didn't say anything. I'm just waiting on the shit she said she had. I walked out of the room to get some fresh air. I sat on the back porch in the swing, the air was chilly, but I am so heated I don't care. The door opened as someone stepped onto the dark porch, I figured it was either Shae or Rod, but it was Emory. She had a blanket in her hands. She sat next to me on the swing and wrapped the purple cotton blanket around us.

"I know the look on your face," she said.

"What look?" I looked at her, but she stared off into the darkness of the back yard.

"He's cheating?" I also began to look out into the yard, "You don't have to say anything because I've been through it."

"I don't deserve this," I broke down. I mean straight bawling my eyes out in front of a girl I've only met hours ago.

"None of us do," she held me, I laid my head on her shoulder. "Sadly, we've fallen in love with the wrong brothers. Shit, Q and Raymond treat their women like royalty, but Rod doesn't, and Chris chooses to follow into his footsteps. Do you know how many people call me stupid for fucking with him?" I shook my head as I dried my tears because I'm stronger than this. "The entire New Bern. I know all the bitches Chris has fucked, tried to fuck, and will fuck. Not because I snoop, but I made him promise to tell me. An ugly truth is always better than a pretty lie. It kills me, but I love him so much. He's my first and my only, but I have chosen to deal with it." She wiped her own tears.

"You're strong, but I refuse to deal with a cheating ass liar."

She shrugged her shoulders, "you can't help who you love, and

Chris loves me. We've never had a problem with any of the bitches coming up to me and I've never had to fight any of them. They just have their little night with my dick and keep it pushing, but Yazzy… Imma fight that bitch. She's a dirty ass bitch that has fucked all of them."

I looked dead into Emory's eyes, "She fucked Rod?"

"Yes, you didn't know?" I shook my head. "Girl, so you don't know why Rod and Q don't get along?" Again, I shook my head. "Yazzy has community pussy, she hangs around them. They are not her homeboys she's just a quick nut. They get high, drunk then horny and she's there like the snake that she is, ready to fuck."

My phone started to buzz with the messages from Teana. "So why the beef between Q and Rod?" I said as I opened the messages.

"Well, …it's a long story. We will have to get together for drinks one night." She leaned over to read the messages with me. Everything Teana said was confirmed. I scrolled down to the numerous pictures of her and Rod, hugged up, kissing, and there was even a video of her sucking his dick. I lost it. Some of the dates were from before he met me, but there were dates from when we were clearly together. He sent her a message claiming I was his friend from out of town and I'm clingy. Emory kept telling me to calm down, but how could I when these past couple of months were a lie?

"I'm done with him," I cried out. The next thirty minutes were spent with Emory trying to console me with no avail. The last time I was this hurt was when I got the news of my parents' accident. I eventually got myself together, I thanked her for everything, this girl has held me up tonight and I'll be forever grateful.

I retrieved my bag from Rod's room. He was lying on his bed when I walked in, he was trying to apologize, his lying ass even dropped a tear. I ignored it all then left. Fuck him. I drove home with tears streaming from my eyes and down my cheeks. This is by far the worst Thanksgiving I've ever had.

CHAPTER 8

Shae and I embarked on the road early Saturday morning to pick up Kennon. Our goal was to check him out of the hospital, then head back to New Bern. I called Aaron to let him know I was coming to Georgia hopefully, I can see him before I leave. The entire drive my mind was on Rod. Those pictures and videos did a number on me. I haven't cried anymore since that Thursday. Rod has been calling my phone nonstop, but I'm not answering. I need way more than an apology, right now apologizing doesn't mean shit. I'm hurt and he needs to understand that. Empathize with me because if the shoes were on the other foot, he wouldn't like the feeling either.

Sam was at the nurse's station when we reached the hospital in Savannah. They've finally moved Kennon from the ICU wing to the regular floor. We gave her a giant hug. I've missed her so much. Sam is close to thirty years old, but she has an old soul. No kids, no husband, its just her and her cats. She loves her job and she treat patients like family. She bakes the best brownies. Sam just cares and everyone needs someone to care for them in the way Sam does while in the hospital.

"Hey girls, I didn't know you were coming today," she said.

"Of course, Kennon says he is ready to get the hell out of here," Shae told her. Kennon has always been an impatient one. He has literally called us every hour of our drive to ask where we were. Between him and Rod calling, my phone is on three percent battery power.

"Well, we hate to see him go, he's been a part of our hospital family for about two years, but we are glad that he's able to walk out of those doors today."

"Amen to that!" I exclaimed. Not too many people are involved in an accident like that and come out on top. It hasn't been easy, he had a lot of odds against him. Some doctors giving up on him, but others believing in the power of God healing him. We gathered all of Kennon's things from his hospital room and he said his final good-byes to the staff. I'm so grateful for what each of them has done for my brother. We ate at a restaurant a couple of blocks from where Aaron works. He came there to see us. I embraced him before he got into the door of the restaurant. We sat at our own table to chat. I told him about the embarrassing situation with Rod. He didn't offer any advice, he just listened and that's all I needed him to do was listen to me vent. I felt better talking to him about it because I know he won't judge me or talk with anybody else about it. Rod's number flashed across my phone's screen and for a split second I thought about answering it, but I didn't. I rather talk with Aaron.

Shae and Kennon joined Aaron and me at our table. We ate and reminisced together. Aaron and Kennon always teased each other. I appreciate Aaron for going to visit Kennon every week. A true best friend. It was time for us to head back to New Bern. I hugged my friend one last time. Back home, the first thing Kennon did was hook his gaming system to his tv. I figured he would be cooped in his room for the rest of the night. I retreated to my own room. Wore out from the road and dealing with Shae's driving. Rod started his calling shit again, "Hello?" I said calmly.

"Si, I've been calling you," he said with attitude.

"I've seen, what's up?"

"I want to see you so we can talk, yo."

"Um...naw I'm good. Everything is pretty clear."

"You haven't heard *me*."

"Fuck, hearing you. You straight played me by fucking with ugly duck-faced looking ass bitches. It's cool though." Everything that comes from his mouth is a lie and at this point I'm done hearing it.

"I didn't play you. I'll never play you."

I scoffed. He really thinks he has me fooled. "Okay Rod, whatever you say."

"Can I come over?"

"No," I said sternly. I don't want to see him right now. Plus, with Kennon being home I do not want to introduce him to Rod while we are on these terms.

"I'm already here," he entered my room. I turned over to see his beautiful face. It makes it so hard to be mad at him while he's staring in my face. He sat beside me.

"Why are you here Rod?" I moved further over in the bed so no part of him could touch me.

"I told you I wanted to talk."

"Go talk to your baby's mother," I snapped. Apart of me wishes he would leave. Another part wished that this didn't even happen so we could go back to how we were before. He has hurt me badly.

He took a deep breath before responding, "She's nothing to me, so stop saying that shit yo."

"I don't care. I'm not in the mood for your lies. See yourself out," I turned over placing my covers over my head.

"I promise I won't lie to you again," I didn't respond I waited for his explanation, "Yes, I have fucked with Teana, but I haven't fucked her since I've been with you. Everything she sent you was old as fuck. I was talking to her before we met but I deaded that shit."

Lie number one, I thought to myself. "Rod," I turned back to him, "I read the messages. You've been talking with her after me. You said I was annoying and shit. I can send you what your bitch sent me."

"I've never said shit like that, Baby you gotta believe that," he pleaded.

"Then that video," no matter how hard I tried to act, the tears started to flow. I promised myself I wouldn't cry anymore.

"Si, that was months ago. I swear to God, I fucking lo..." He began to sob. "Man, fuck," he jumped from the bed to punch the wall, leaving a small dent. "Yo, I've never fallen for a girl this fast. This shit is scary, and I know I fucked up," he leaned into me, his tears dripped on my face, "I promise, I'll never make you feel like this ever again, yo," he whispered. I sat up to wipe his tears, "I never want to be the reason for these," he said while wiping my tears. He kissed me so passionately, then we embraced for at least two minutes. It's still a lot I didn't get to mention, but as of right now…I don't care about any bitches he's fucked before me. I love him and I know he loves me. Nobody's perfect, men and women make mistakes, and I forgive him completely. As the sun was coming up, Rod laid behind me snuggled to my body. "Are you mine again?" He asked.

"I'm always yours," I smiled. I decided to skip class today, I wanted to spend more time with Rod. I emailed my professors informing them, well lying to them about being in Georgia with my brother. Luckily, they were understanding.

Rod awoke me with morning head. I like his gestures of winning me back, but I'm all his. He's not quite out of the doghouse yet. I muffled my moans until I couldn't any longer. He licked me below so lovingly, a tear escaped my eye. I came for the second time this morning. I was overcome with ecstasy as I moaned his name. I straddled Rod, gyrating against him. Rod and I have talked about me being on top, but truth be told I'm so afraid to be in total control. The fact of him watching me and actually doing it right is frightening. My palms began to become sweaty. My eyes never left his eyes as I slowly slid down the shaft of his penis. I held onto the headboard to maintain my balance, I rode him, he gripped my ass the entire time guiding me. His beautiful face scrunched as he came inside of me. I shivered from my own climax and then I collapsed in his arms, he held me tight. I had a huge smile on my face as we cuddled and watched a movie. He dozed off to sleep and I watched him. His naked tattooed body in my bed, I placed small kisses down the center of his chiseled chest, he awoke. "Mmmm," he cupped my face, bringing me closer. "I love you so much Baby," he kissed me.

"And I love you." Rod stretched before grabbing his bag with his weed in it. He smoked as I worked on homework. Rod and I got dressed to start our day.

"Before we go to Greenville, I need to stop by JP's crib," Rod said. I rolled my eyes, I don't like JP, he's sketchy and talks too much shit. Plus, he acts like Rod *has* to come to see him every day. I put my hair in a messy bun. As usual, when we pulled up in front of JP's apartment, it was flooded with niggas. "Are you coming in?" He looked over at me.

I looked at him like he was crazy, "No, it is way too many niggas out there," I shook my head.

"C'mon, plus I don't know how long it's gonna take." It's below sixty degrees and these niggas out here standing like its summertime and in front of somebody's else shit. Where they do that at? I bypassed all of them niggas without so much of a hey or eye contact. Of course, Rod dapped every single last one of them, they all lined up like he was a celebrity. JP's apartment reeked of weed, and I do not want to smell like that shit all day. I sat beside one of their friends on the small couch. They were doing what they do best, playing the game while smoking weed. I spoke to the men in the house, JP eyed me seductively like he always does. "What's good, bro?" Rod asked him, he sat on the stool.

"Coolin, aye Rico, show 'em, bro." Rico came from the kitchen with a Ziploc bag filled with small bags with some white shit in it.

"What the fuck is this?" Rod asked as I was thinking the exact same thing.

"That's what he gave me bro," JP answered him.

"Where the fuck that nigga at?"

"Around the way."

"Iight, bet," Rod said as he put the bag in his coat.

"What is that?" I asked. They all looked at me and shared a laugh.

"Ain't nothing but a little snow," JP stated.

Snow, I thought to myself. What the fuck is that.

"Let's go," Rod said to me, he seemed aggravated.

"What's snow?" I asked him once we were back in the car.

"Seriously?" He questioned. He put the bag carefully under his seat. I nodded my head, I'm not from the hood and I don't know their lingo. "It's coke," he said plainly.

Pause…. this nigga got real live coke right now. I figured it was some type of drug. "What are you doing with it?"

"What you mean?" He smirked. He started the car, then pulled off.

"You heard me."

"It's mine," he made a turn on River road.

"What do you mean, yours? Do you do that shit?" I glared directly at him, he acted as if he was paying more attention to the road than to our current conversation. You would've thought I asked the world's hardest question.

"I sell it."

"You…. sell it? To who? So, you're a…." I paused as I collected my thoughts, "*drug dealer?*"

He pulled into the fast-food chain parking lot in Vanceboro. I had his full attention now. He unbuckled his seat belt then looked at me, "Yes, baby, I sell dope. You seriously did not know this?"

"Really Rod? How was I supposed to know if you didn't tell me?" Did he expect me to find out from the streets? I don't even hang out like that, and it is not like the people I do hang around will offer up that information. 'Hey, your boyfriend is a drug dealer,' said nobody ever. I guess Daddy was right about niggas who hang in The Bricks.

"Is it a problem?"

"Yes, I don't want that around me," I pouted.

"It's never around you. This is the first time I've had it near you."

"That's not the point. We have drugs in the car and we're riding all the way to Greenville. I don't feel safe," I folded my arms.

"What do you want me to do, Si?"

"I don't know, get rid of it and I can't believe you're a fucking drug dealer."

He sighed heavily, looking out the window. "Si, I can't do that. When we get back, I'll handle it."

"No, take me home."

"Naw," he pulled off heading towards Greenville again. "If you're gonna be with me, you have to calm your ass down and stop being so paranoid. I won't let anything happen to you."

I sulked in my seat, "I'm not paranoid," I mumbled under my breath. Once in Greenville, shopping made me forgot about the drugs in his car. We shopped in the mall, Rod brought us matching sneakers. He also brought me some outfits, he is spoiling me, and I love it. We walked hand in hand throughout the mall, Rod leads me into the store that carried sex toys. We were like kids, giggling and touching everything. I made my way to the vibrators.

"Get one, I want to watch as you play with yourself," he said into my ear. I laughed it off, I've never pleasured myself and I definitely wasn't going to do it in front of him. I admit I got wet from the thought of it. Fuck it, I picked out a slim green one. I found myself excited, and I can tell Rod is too, but time will tell if I get the courage to use it or not. I heard all girls are supposed to own a vibrator, you know…for the hard times.

Finally, we ate at a steakhouse, I ordered so much food then ended up needing to go plates. I sent a text to Emory on when and where to meet up, I like her, she's cool. A bit gullible but a really down to earth chick.

"Can I ask you something?" We were making our way back to his car.

"You can ask me anything."

"Have you had sex with Yazzy?"

"Yeah."

I waited for more words to escape his lips, but nothing. "Really?" I wanted to be mad so bad, but we've been having such a good day.

"Would you like for me to give you a list of all the bitches I've fucked?"

"Hell yeah, especially if it consists of females I fuck with," I put the bags in the back seat, then climbed on the passenger side.

He smirked, "The past is the past. I'm fucking you, and frankly, that's all that matters to me. Do you like when I'm fucking *you*?"

"Rod!" I rolled my eyes.

"Answer my question."

"Yes."

"Yes, what?" He asked playfully and seductively.

"I like it when you fuck me, but I *love it* when you make love to me."

"Oh yeah?!" He licked his lips. "What about when I eat your pussy?"

"Rod! Drive!"

"What?! We're just having a conversation." He rubbed my inner thigh, "I know you love that shit."

Rod dropped me off home, he had to make a run. I'm guessing to take the drugs to where they needed to be. Emory was waiting for me in my room. I texted Kendra letting her know it was cool for Emory to be there. The good thing about living with Kendra in New Bern is that she may not know everyone, but she has heard about them. Sometimes she can tell you their mother's or father's name, older sibling's name, or even their auntie or uncle. New Bern is small, and the people are connected some type of way.

"Hey, look at you looking all cute," she said complimenting my outfit.

"Thanks, girl," she was sitting on my giraffe printed rug. I threw my purse on my bed before joining her. "So, I found out Rod sell cocaine."

"What? You didn't know?"

"Hell no, I was so fucking mad too."

"Girl," she said as she pulled out a pink and black pencil case. She retrieved a gold back of blunts, a small green bag of weed, and a pink grinder. "Everybody in New Bern knows, can I borrow your trash can?" I gave her the trash can, she ground the weed and rolled it with so much finesse, I was impressed.

"Nobody told me though," I pouted.

"I'm sorry honey, I thought you knew."

"No, it is not your fault, it's Rod's. He should've told me way before today."

"If it makes you feel any better, I was upset when Chris told me too." She retrieved a pink lighter from the case, "Is it cool if I smoke this?"

"Sure, go ahead. Chris sells too?" I was so tuned in to her.

"Yep, and Ray and Q. It's like a family affair," she chuckled as she inhaled the blunt. She laid completely flat on the carpet. I didn't even know this girl smoked. She extended the blunt, I declined. "Come on Siah, I can't face off with you here. I'll feel bad. Plus, dealing with the boyfriends we have, a little weed helps." I took a pull of the blunt and immediately blew it out. "No, honey, you're wasting it. Let me show you." She took the blunt from me, "Pull it," she pulled from the blunt, the end glowed red, "take a deep breath, hold it in for two to three seconds." She held it in, "then blow it out," smoke came out her mouth and nose. "Now try it," I did as she instructed, and I could feel myself get more relaxed. She then advised me to take at least five puffs before passing it back to her. I began to feel woozy, not drunk woozy, but something different. A feeling I can't quite describe, but I like it. Once we finished the blunt, she put the small piece on top of a soda bottle she had. Now we both rested on the carpet.

"Emory?"

"Yes, honey?"

"We should do this more often," we laughed loud and uncontrolled.

Rod walked in, "What's up?" He removed his jacket then sat on the bed.

"Oh, hey baby," I said. Emory and I laughed again.

"Em, What the fuck yo?" He said, kicking off his shoes.

"What?!" She laughed.

"Why the fuck would you get her high?"

"Chill baby, Emory and I are bonding….and I'm hungry."

"Noooo, don't eat. It brings your high down," she informed me, "Rod, where is your brother?"

"I don't know, call him."

"I have, but he's not answering. He knows how I get when I smoke."

Rod pointed across the room, "Si has a big ass computer over there. Have fun," he laughed.

"Whatever," she sat up to find her phone and I climbed into bed with Rod. He grabbed my ass, pulling me closer to him. Instantly wet. While Emory was fussing with Chris, Rod's cool hand was sliding into my panties. He massaged my pussy.

"Emory's here," I moaned quietly as I closed my eyes taking in the pleasure.

"She's not looking," he continued to rub my clit with his fingertips.

"Damn, you're drenched," he whispered as he dipped his finger in my honey jar.

"I'll be at your house. Be there in ten minutes. Love you, bye." I heard Emory say. I threw the covers across Rod and me, "I'm heading out, I'll see you two later," she gathered her things.

"I'll walk you out," I offered.

"No, I'm good. Hit me up tomorrow."

When she walked out, Rod finished what he started. "Take your clothes off," I did. Rod removed his clothes. "Where's our toy?" I pointed to the dresser beside my bed. I put it there so it was close by and that's one dresser Shae doesn't go in to steal clothes. "Lay down," he licked his fingers, then grabbed the ready to use with new batteries vibrator. Rod put it against my clit, I bit my bottom lip. He moved it and suckled on my throbbing clit. "I want to watch you use it baby," I don't know what I'm going to do, but how hard could it be? If I can't pleasure myself how am I able to tell him how I like to be touched? I took the vibrator in my hand and rubbed it on my clit. I closed my eyes as I turned the vibrator on. I peeped at Rod, his dick was hard. I coated the vibrator with my juices, and I imagined it as Rod's penis. I slowly slid it into my wetness, I gripped my titty as I slid the vibrator in and out of my tight pussy. I shuddered as I amplified my speed. My moans beamed off the walls. Rod was also pleasuring himself from the sight of me. I was so fucking turned on and on the brink of a climax. I spread my legs wider, I kept the vibrator at a steady pace. I rotated my hips in small circles. "That's right baby fuck that pussy," he grunted, he came on his hand and I came soon after. I rubbed my clit with my fingers, tossing the vibrator to the side. Rod grabbed a towel to wipe his hand. I continued to rub my clit until Rod came back, he moved my hand then entered me deeply. He thrust in me each time going deeper than before, "Rub your clit," he instructed. I rubbed it just as swiftly as his dick entered me. I shuddered as I came, gripping the sheets. He slid out of me, "I want you to taste what I taste," he said quietly. He licked his lips. I know what he means, but I'm not quite ready for that, but right now I'm so horny I'm down for whatever. He laid on the bed, I leaned over, my face near his crotch.

I stared at his hard dick, mmm, did it look delicious. A mixture of our juices glistening from it, I place my tongue over the head of his penis, making it wet with my saliva. I closed my eyes as I took it in my mouth. I repositioned between his legs, laying on my stomach. I swirled my wet tongue around the tip again, then drew it into my mouth again I bobbed my head rhythmically. He moaned out, that turned me on, even more, he grasped the back of my head. I took him deeper into my mouth, gagging a little. I imagined his dick as being my favorite lollipop. The more I sucked the more I liked it. His moans were driving me wild. I continued until he came in my mouth, I swallowed the thick, salty load. It wasn't as bad as I imagined it to be, I've heard men's cum was an acquired taste and I now agree. It's different from anything I've tasted before, but not bad. "You swallowed it?" Rod asked. I nodded my head and his dick rose again. "Turn around," he instructed. With my ass in the air Rod entered me from behind, he went so deep I gasped for air. He held onto my waist tightly as he glided in and out of me.

"Oooooh…. Rod, I'm about to cum," I moaned loudly. Deeper and harder he went, I shivered as I neared the ultimate success of sex.

"Cum for me Baby," and I did. I came all over his dick. My juices soaked the bed. We flopped onto the bed. I toyed with the sweat beads on his lightly haired chest. "I love the way you moan my name," he whispered. I smiled. My high was definitely gone, but I enjoyed it while it lasted. I liked how it made me feel. He smoked from his bowl and I went to sleep.

I had a missed call and voicemail from Emory. She was crying and that really upset me. What the fuck did Chris do this time? Rod was asleep so I went into the bathroom to call her back. "Hey, what's wrong?"

"Meet me at Yazzy's in five minutes," she said calmly as she ended the call. Yazzy's? I questioned myself. I like Emory and all, but I'm not getting into any beef she has with Yazzy. Just because Yazzy and I are not on speaking terms does not mean I don't still have love for the girl. Even if she did fuck my man before and didn't tell me about it. But I do want to be there for Emory. I put on my sweatpants with my Effingham County High School hoodie. Emory pulled up a minute after I did. She signaled for me to get out of the car. I tried to read her face, but she was emotionless and surprisingly calm.

"Why are we here?" I asked her, I shivered from the cold, dry air. She didn't utter a word, I followed her as she speed walked to Yazzy's front door. I tried to grab her hand before she could knock, but I was unsuccessful. She bammed on the door so hard you would've thought she was trying to break the door down.

Yazzy opened the door, looked Emory up and down then looked at me confused, but I don't have the answers for her. "What?!" She asked us plainly, I could tell she was annoyed, but what was she going to do?

Emory had a disgusted look on her face, "I'm gonna say this one fucking time, leave Chris alone," she stepped closer to Yazzy's face, "those late-night phone calls and lame-ass texts *will* stop today," Emory meant business.

"And if they don't?" Yazzy stood her ground which I knew she would. I only stood there. It's too cold for all this. Besides, what could I say? This isn't my business. Call me moral support.

"Then I'm gonna beat your ass. Point. Blank. Period. I'm tired of you."

Yazzy laughed in Emory's face, "Maybe you should tell *your man* to stay away from me."

Emory swung hitting Yazzy in her jaw. Yazzy stumbled back, shocked. Yazzy pulled Emory's hair slinging her onto the ground. These bitches are really going at it all in the kitchen of Yazzy's apartment. I tried pulling Emory off Yazzy, but her little ass is strong. I called Rod frantically. Emory kicked Yazzy in the head and stomach with her knee-high studded boots. Emory was getting the best of her and I felt bad for my old friend.

"Em, stop!" I shouted, but she ignored me.

"Siah, get this bitch off of me," Yazzy cried out. Emory punched her in her mouth then started swinging at her while she was on the ground. Yazzy tried to block the blows.

I drifted off into my own world. I wanted to help, but my body told me to keep my distance. In a way the beating Emory was giving to her was for me too. Yazzy deserved what she was getting. I love her, but I love Rod more. She's been my friend for years and I can't believe she would push us together knowing she'd sex with him. What satisfaction does bitches get out of setting their friends up with niggas they've previously fucked? That shit is crazy to me. Then on the other hand what brothers would take turns fucking the same whore? I wonder if Rod was ever in love with her. I'm so torn right now. A girl I've known forever who has lied to me for as long as I knew her and a young girl who has kept it real with me since day one. My loyalty should lie with Yazzy, but it doesn't. I didn't like the scene that was before me, but I support it in a way. Honestly, Emory is fighting over a man who is still going to lay down with Yazzy and other females at the end of the day, but I respect her for standing her ground and letting these hoes know she's not to be fucked with.

Chris suddenly ran in through the same door Emory and I came in. He quickly snatched Emory up like she was a sheet of paper, "Chill," he yelled in her face backing her against the fridge. Emory looked like she wanted to swing on him, but he had her arms pinned. Yazzy got up from the floor with her bundles all over the place, she had a bloody nose and lip. I could see a knot was also forming on her head. I leaned against the counter adjacent from the scene. Emory yelled for Chris to get off her, he did but he stayed close.

"Get her out my house," Yazzy said as she wiped her mouth with her shirt. Yazzy began to cry, she must have felt the sting from the split of her lip, "NOW!" She screamed.

"All ya'll calm the fuck down, what is the problem?" He asked as if he didn't know. Rod then walked into the apartment and stood beside me, he looked pissed.

"You fucking this bitch is the problem," Emory fixed her hair and Yazzy was still crying.

"Yo, bro. This shit ain't cool," Rod said to Chris.

"Rod, please get her out of here," Yazzy pleaded with Rod.

"Oh, the bitch wants to cry now. Earlier she thought shit was funny," Emory tried to go after the flinching Yazzy again.

"Em, Babe, calm the fuck down," Chris spat pinning her against the refrigerator harder than before.

"No, Chris, fuck you! I'm fucking done. She can have your stupid ass. Now get the fuck off me," Emory struggled to be free.

"I don't want her, I want you," Chris dropped to his knees hugging onto Emory's legs. "Bae, I'm sorry," he too, began to weep.

"Rod," Emory spoke through clenched teeth. Rod pulled Chris from Emory just enough for her to move. "It's over," she stood at the back door.

"EMORY!" Chris punched the refrigerator. Yazzy retreated to her living room. My heart ached for Chris, but he caused all this shit on himself.

"Come on Siah," Emory said walking out. Chris tried to walk out, but Rod stood in his way. Defeated, Chris knew not to challenge his big brother. He hung his head as he walked to the other room.

I started to walk out the door as well, but Rod grabbed my arm, pulling me back. "Why did you let this go down?" He questioned.

I looked at him confused, "Are you blaming me for this? I can't control Emory. I simply met her over here as she asked, I had no idea this was going to happen."

"Come on, Si. You knew this shit wasn't gonna end good. When she called you, you should've woken me."

"No, I…." I started to say.

"Bye, Yo. I'll get with you later," Rod walked off into the living room.

I can't believe Rod is mad with me. When I got into Emory's car she had the heat blasting. Tears were pouring from her small face, "Are you okay?"

"Hell no, but I will be," she wiped the tears from her cheeks, "Are you free later?"

"Yes, of course."

"I'll text you. I need to talk, but I need to get myself together first."

"I'm here for you, just like you were for me." She backed out the parking lot, we pulled into the biggest park in New Bern that overlooked the river.

"I'm really done, Siah. Chris and I've been together for six years and we've never, not once broke up even when I found out he was cheating, I stayed. But I've had enough," she stared out the window at the people throwing stale bread to the ducks.

"I can tell he loves you," I told her. I'm not taking up for him, but from my view of things, he cares for her deeply.

"But he doesn't appreciate me nor respects me. My dad has always told me to never let a man disrespect me. I've dealt with it for way too long," she reclined her seat back as far as it could go. Her father sounds a lot like mine, and the words he spoke are true. "This is too much," she threw her hands over her eyes.

"I promise, it's gonna be okay."

For the next thirty minutes, she shared her feelings and I gave her my undivided attention. After all the tears, darkness fell upon us. She drove me back to my car then drove away. I don't blame her for not wanting to stare at Yazzy's apartment. Rod's car was still parked beside mine, but Chris' car was gone. I called Rod, but he didn't answer. The voicemail came up way too soon, so I know he sent my call to voicemail. I should walk my ass up to her door to cuss him out, but I won't. Imma take my ass home. Rod can be so childish, I thought to myself as I showered. Why is he even mad at me? I stayed up until midnight waiting for him to call or text me back, but nothing. At least Shae was having a good night because she and Raymond were next door having loud as sex again. The shit is annoying as hell, but I wonder if they can hear Rod and me. I put my headphone in my ear then call Rod again.

"What's up?" He answered. An R&B song was playing in the background.

"Hey! Where are you?"

"I'm chillin yo, what's up?" He sounded drunk.

"Are you coming over tonight?"

"Naw, yo. Imma crash at Yazzy's shit. She's still fucked up about earlier."

"So? What does that have to do with you?"

"She's my nigga," he slurred.

"No, she's a bitch you've fucked."

He laughed, "you're wildin."

Rod is really pissing me off. "Are you coming or not? I have class tomorrow and I need to be sleep."

"Yes, I will be there. Give me ten minutes."

The next morning, no Rod. I got ready for class. I'm mad because he could've kept it real with me from the jump if he wasn't going to come last night. I'm glad I didn't stay up waiting for him. Am I a joke to him? Why does he continue to hang around her? What is it about her? Gosh, I sound insecure as hell. Even though I am, I can't show him that I'm jealous of their relationship. I just don't understand it at all. Tell me what's up and don't keep me in the dark. Maybe it's time for me to fall back. I don't know where I stand with my own boyfriend and that is so sad. One minute we are hot then the next minute we are cold. When it's good, it's good. When it's bad and he doesn't like what I do then it's the end of the world, and he shuts me out. I cannot stay mad at him for too long, but he can stay mad at me for a while. That's ridiculous! My focus is school and getting to where I want to be in life. I'm still deciding on what I want to do after I graduate, and Rod is becoming a distraction. I've always heard that a person will have at least one heartbreak in their lifetime, but why? Why would the one we love break our hearts if they claim to love us? Love is not supposed to hurt. I genuinely believe Rod loves me, but it's like he doesn't always allow himself to get that close to me, emotionally. He's been hurt by girls in the past, but he needs to know that I will never hurt him. If both of us develop that mindset of not wanting to intentionally hurt each other then we will be good, right?

I met Emory for lunch at the same authentic Mexican restaurant Erica and Drea took me to. She looked way better than yesterday, a little too good for a girl who just had her heart ripped out and stomped on by a nigga. We munched on the complimentary tortilla chips and salsa before placing our entrée orders. "You look good," I complimented her. I like her sense of style, she dresses up no matter the occasion.

"Thanks, Boo, so do you, I always love your hair," I wished I felt as good as I looked, I smiled as I touched my hair flowing down my back with an old school banana clip. I had to dig through so much stuff to find this clip.

"How are you feeling?"

"Better now," she sat back. "Chris and I had a long conversation last night." She paused. "Girl...when I tell you that nigga can lie, whoo." she rolled her eyes. "I let him eat my pussy and then I left his house. I don't want him anymore."

We shared a laugh. Baby girl is turning ruthless, maybe I can learn a thing or two from her.

"I'm glad *your* night was good. I haven't talked to Rod."

"Let me guess? He was at Yazzy's house? Dirty ass house at that. I didn't know that bitch lived like that." We cackled again.

I nodded, "I want him to respect why I don't want him near her."

"Be careful Babe. I don't want you to end up in the same situation as me."

"But what can I do?"

"Demand respect, I've failed to make Chris respect me and our relationship because I was so caught up in love." I nodded in agreement. No more letting Rod do what he wants, if he wants to be in this relationship with me then things must change. Emory and I parted ways. I called Rod when I got home.

"What's good?" He asked sleepily. It's 2:00, I know he is not just now waking up. I could feel myself getting furious. I took a deep breath. I'm learning that when a girl gives herself to someone, they start losing interest. He's not even trying anymore. The little voice in the back of my head is telling me to make him try. Shit, act like you still love me.

"Are you still at Yazzy's house?"

"No, Baby, I'm home..." he yawned, "Slide through." I smiled. He made me forget I was mad at him before. I gathered my bookbag, threw some snacks in then jumped in my car heading towards his house. I let myself in, as I headed to Rod's room, I ran into Q.

"What's up?" he asked. I tried to avoid having a conversation with him since Rod didn't act favorably the last time.

"Hey, Q." I started off to Rod's room.

"He's not here,"

I turned to face him, "What do you mean? I literally just spoke with him ten minutes ago."

"He had to make a run real fast. Want to wait with me in the den until he gets back?" I was reluctant, but I waited with him. I sat on the white leather sofa in the 'den'. The room is a bonus room down the hall from Rod's room. This is my first time being in here, but from the looks of it, they use this room a lot. Half-naked girls' posters graced the wall, a large flat screen tv, and a small island served as the bar. Bottles of alcohol were stocked in the cabinet. A glass table sat in the middle of the room by the couches. I took my jacket off, hanging it on the coat rack behind the door. "Are you thirsty?" I nodded. He retrieved a wine cooler from the mini fridge behind the island. He opened it before handing it to me. Such a gentleman! I laughed to myself though, because how many females have they had in here to keep wine coolers stocked? He sat in the other chair then pulled the table closer to him. He tossed the remote to me. I flipped through the channels. He retrieved a small bag from his pocket, it resembles the cocaine that Rod had earlier this week. I watched as he emptied the contents on the table then proceed to chop it with a razor. I watched him closely, I guess he felt my eyes on him and the curiosity upon my face. "What's wrong?"

I shook my head. He's about to snort this shit right in front of me. I can't look away. He snorted it in one whiff using a tightly rolled dollar bill. He sniffed loudly, throwing his head back. "You want some?" He sat forward. I looked at him like he was crazy and shook my head. This nigga just snorted a line in front of me like he had no shame, is this real? Am I dreaming? I downed the current wine cooler, then went to get me another one, I downed that one too. Q pulled three bundles of coke from beside the couch then set it on the table.

"You sell too right?" I asked blankly remembering the information given to me by Emory.

He smirked, "Who do you think put my little brothers on?"

I shrugged, "So you use and sell it?"

"You make it sound like I'm a crackhead or some shit," he laughed. "I have to test the quality of my shit before I put it out on the streets."

I didn't know what else to say, I have so many questions, but I rather ask Rod.

"Yo," Rod entered the room. "What's up, Baby?" He kissed my lips. I breathed in his scent as he sat beside me. "What we looking like," he said to Q. They're on speaking terms now? Not trying to fight each other? Their relationship is weird.

"We're straight, what did you do about that shit Daniel pulled?"

"I handled it," Rod took a small amount of the coke and rubbed it on his gums. "Hm, shit. This from Zo's connect?"

"Yeah, bro. Good shit! But that shit that Daniel pulled cannot happen again."

"He knows. Enough talk, we'll link up later. I need to spend some time with my girl." I beamed inside. Although, it is nice that they included me in their business talk. I kicked off my boots and tossed them across his room. He sat in his chaise.

"Do you even want to be together?"

"What? Where the fuck did that come from?"

"I've been thinking and the shit that you do makes me think that you don't want us anymore. I won't stand for you disrespecting and pushing me away."

"Disrespect you? When? I've disrespected a lot of girls, but not you. I'll never do that shit to you."

"I don't want you anywhere near Yazzy," I stated. He laughed slightly and it irritated me. I am serious and he needs to understand that. I folded my arms across my large breasts. "I'm going to leave and not come back if the disrespect continues."

"Here you go saying that again."

"It's true, it's disrespectful for you to continue to be around someone that *your girl* asks you not to be around."

"Si, what you don't understand is that I trap out her crib. We make most of our money from her shit. Asking me to stop going there is like asking me to say, 'fuck my money' and I can't do that."

"Well, then you can't be with me." I waited for his response.

"We're going to be together, no matter what. I need you to at least meet me halfway." He came closer to me, I kept my arms folded. He nibbled on my neck, "How about, I won't hang over as much and I don't stay out too late." He said between kisses.

"Midnight?" I moaned softly. I melted right into his arms. I draped my arms around his shoulders. "I want you next to me every night."

"You never have to worry about that. I'll make my way to you always." He picked me up and I wrapped my legs around him. He lay me gently on the king-sized bed. I love you so much, Si," he whispered.

"I love you too."

Compromise, if you aren't willing to compromise in your relationship then why be in one? I'm sure my parents made tons of compromises. I remember one in particular when I was twelve years old and we were driving home from one of Kennon's recreation basketball games in Screven County. Daddy asked us all what we preferred to eat because once we arrive at home its lights out. Shae and I let Kennon pick the restaurant because his team had won the game. Of course, being the 9-year-old active kid, he was, he chose the most popular fast-food chain. Mom didn't care for the restaurant, but she didn't utter a single word in disagreement. She sat in silence. My daddy knew how she felt about the food which is why he drove to a nearby Chinese restaurant to order her favorite plate as she stayed with us at the restaurant. She had no idea he was going to do that for her which made his gesture so sweet. The look on her face was priceless. My dad was very tight with money and also hated making multiple stops. It was either eat where we stop or don't eat at all, but he compromised for Mom. That's love. Two people that want to be together and fight for their love and bond will compromise all the time for the well-being of their relationship. I will always compromise the small and big things with Rod if he's willing to do the same for me.

CHAPTER 9

"Imma kill his ass," were the words spoken by Shae. She paced back and forth in my room. Watching her pace reminded of the night Officer Moore informed us of the accident. Shae paced all night long, emotionless. This pacing was a result of a phone call from our first cousin, Dimanasia. Growing up we were so close with Dimanasia but living so many miles apart has hindered our relationship. If I want intel on Rod, I know I can go to Dimanasia for all the scoop, but Rod and I are in such a good space right now and I don't want to ruin it.

I looked up from my homework, "What happened?" She continued to pace as if she didn't hear my question. Shae always shuts down when she has a problem. I can tell she wants to talk about it, so just talk dammit. A good minute passed before she acknowledged me.

"Did Rod say anything about me and Raymond?" I wanted to be sarcastic and say yeah because Rod and I sit around and talk about her and Raymond all day. We don't pay attention to anybody's relationship.

I replied with a simple, "No."

"Of course not, anyway. I found some stank ass thongs under his pillow," she paced with her fist tightly clenched. "So, I trashed his room, trying to see what else the bitch left over there. He convinced me that the tongs must have been Erica's. Dimanasia just told me she saw him with some bitch in The Bricks," anger controlled her words, but she needs more than Dimanasia's word because sometimes cuz isn't credible.

"Just talk to Raymond."

"I will and you need to talk to Rod."

"Why?" I glared at her awaiting an answer, I rubbed the inside of my palm. She walked out of the room, what is she talking about? I hate riddles and I hate when people bring up shit and don't finish the thought. Misery loves company. Tomorrow is my last day of class before winter break starts. I'm so excited and anxious to spend every minute of every day with Rod. I put my notebook and laptop away. Finally done. I've been working on papers all day. I sent Rod a sweet text and he texted back saying he will be over very soon. Butterflies formed in my stomach.

I prepared for our night, I paid close attention to my honey jar. I shave daily, I like to keep my pussy hairs to no hairs at all. Rod likes it like that too. I made sure the water hit every aspect of my body. The warmth soothed me. I rubbed the soap all over my body with my pink pouf. I started to envision Rod's sexy body. I hung the pouf on the shower holder. My hands wandered over my breast, I squeezed them gently. I realized I was a lot hornier than I thought. I got out of the shower, wet inside and out. Rod was standing in the door frame with my towel in his hand. This man is beyond sexy and he showed up just in time. He is so high. I got so lucky with him. Months ago, I would've quickly covered my body, but now I don't have that urge. It's funny how much losing my virginity has matured me.

He stared at me, taking in my image like he hasn't seen me naked before. "Come here," he said in his deep, low tone. He picked me up, my wet body pressed against the coldness of his coat. We shared a passionate, lustful kiss. I tasted the alcohol on his tongue. He lay me on my unmade bed. Gently removed his coat as he continued to kiss me. His soft lips are like a piece of your favorite candy and I can't get enough.

"Rod, can we talk?"

"Mmm…yes…after. I need this right now," he begun to finger me.

I moaned deeply, closing my eyes. His hardened dick pressed against me, "Rod…" I moaned as I tried to push his hand away from me.

"Si, stop," he whispered. He freed his dick which took the place of his fingers. He moaned as he pumped inside of me, "Fuck, your pussy is so good," he fell in complete ecstasy. His eyes remained closed as he did his thing. He hit all the right spots of my body. "Whose pussy is this?" He asked as he increased his speed.

"Yours," I moaned into his ear."

"Mmmm…. hmmmm," he grunted, our breathing intensified. "I love you," he grunted again as he came. He collapsed alongside me. He laid against my pillow, I straddled him. I want more. I pulled his shirt over his head and ran my tongue against his neck. I continue to place lingering kisses on his neck and chest. He moaned lightly, "You wanted to talk, right?" I continued what I was doing, talking can wait when this sexy specimen is before my eyes. I placed kisses all down his body until I got to my favorite part. I stared into his eyes as I devoured his dick in my warm mouth for the second time in my life. I proceed to suck him, my eyes never left him and that drove him a step closer to his climax. My eager tongue made its way to his testicles. I suckled on them one at a time, allowing my tongue to leave a trail of saliva between the two. I let each one invade the inside of my mouth. I swirled my tongue on them keeping them from moving so much with the hand I was gripping his dick with, I turned my attention back to the shaft. Now giving it my undivided attention. I moaned as he moaned, shit I'm enjoying it just as much as he is. I placed kisses up and down the shaft. The way I kiss his lips is the same way I kiss his dick. I moved my hair out the way as I continued to give him all that was in me. I took it in deeper than ever before and even slapped his dick against my tongue. I took my time because I want him to enjoy every minute of this blow job. I wanted every inch of his penis coated with my saliva. He came so hard it was dripping from the sides of my mouth, I swallowed every drop. "Let me see," he said to me. I stuck out my tongue showing him that his cum was no longer in my mouth. I love how I can be nasty with Rod. "That's my girl," he said as he pulled me to him. He moved the stray hair from my face.

I felt Rod's side of the bed the next morning, but he wasn't by my side. Insecurity crept in. I felt his side again and realized it was cold, which means he hasn't been there for a while, I stared at the dark ceiling. I can't keep dealing with this, I checked my phone. No texts or calls.

"What's wrong?" I heard his voice and my doubts and insecurities went away. I sat up. The moonlight glowed in my room. He was sitting by my window.

"Nothing," I lied. "What are you doing?" He had his phone in his hand.

"Looking up recipes to cook for you," I blushed. I covered my body from the chill. "Get dressed."

"Why, where do you want to go?"

"Anywhere but here," he was full of energy.

"Now? Rod, I can't. I have an exam in like two hours."

"So, you can't do shit with your man?" He started to get aggravated.

"Wait, what? Yes, but we will have to go later," I love how spontaneous he is, but I have responsibilities.

"Naw, fuck it," he spat. "I'll be back tomorrow."

"Tomorrow? Rod what is wrong with you." I felt so bad telling him no, but what kind of person would I be if I missed my finals? I would have to take the entire class over, and I'll be damned if I do that.

"Nothing, yo. I gotta make a run." He left. No kiss. No goodbye. Just left. I peeked from my window watching which direction he went. I quickly dressed then headed to Shae's car to follow him, I need to know exactly what kind of run he had to make. He's not about to have me looking stupid. I went about 50 miles per hour in a 25 trying to keep up with him. I didn't want to follow too close, because at this hour it's not many cars out and I don't want to get caught being crazy. He stopped at JP's house, late night/early morning there were people hanging around the apartment. One female ran up towards him, but he disregarded her attempt to talk to him. That made me smile. I watched closely as he disappeared into the apartment. My nerves are so shot right now. He exited the apartment with a book bag. He put the bag in the back seat then drove off. His next stop was Yazzy's. She ran outside before his car was even parked. No coat, just a tank top and pajama pants. Ratchet hoe. He stepped from his car and she hugged him. He gripped her ass then handed her the bag from the backseat. She smiled saying something to him, he said something back. Too bad I can't read lips. He drove off again, but I waited until Yazzy's door was closed before I followed. We traveled to Jamescity, passed his house. He parked in the driveway of a brick house. Rod was making moves like it was daytime and ain't nothing open this time of the morning, but legs. He walked up to the well-lit door stoop to ring the doorbell. A female opened the door, she seemed to be fussing him out and I could see him laughing then start to walk back towards his car. I peered closer to watch the scene. Luckily, a trailer park was across from the house, I parked at a trailer as if I lived there. I then see another female push past the first female at the door, so she could catch up with Rod. She tried to pull him back towards the house, but he wouldn't budge. He kept pointing to the other girl, who was still fussing. Rolling her neck and pointing her finger. The girl with Rod wrapped her arms around his neck then kissed his lips….my lips. I gasped as a tear escaped my eye. My broken heart was thumping so loud in my ear. I didn't care what time it was, I called Emory.

"Siah?" She said in a deep, sleepy voice, "What's going on?"

"I followed Rod," I burst out in tears.

"Where are you?" I took minutes to let my emotions out. I'm numb from what I just saw. I heard Emory, but answering her question is the hard part.

"SIAH!" She yelled into my ear. I dropped my location. Emory showed up moments later. She parked in the driveway behind Rod's car. She motioned for me to come to her.

"I'm not knocking on these people's door at this time of the morning," I said when I approached her.

"Then why are you here? We're handling this shit now." I reluctantly approached the door with her. She knocked on the door and rang the doorbell. I'm so scared, but I must toughen up and quick because I'm not about to let these bitches see this weak and vulnerable side of me. The door swung open. The girl that answered the door for Rod stood there, "What the fuck? Do you know what time it is?"

"Fuck all that, where the fuck is Rod at?" Emory spat.

"Down the hall with Teana, why?" She said with attitude and I realized that this was the bitch waitress from when Rod and I first met.

"We need him!"

"What are ya'll some fiends or some shit? It's late as fuck."

"Fiends?" Emory smirked and looked at me then back at the girl, "Bitch, you got about one second to get that nigga or you gone get laid out."

She sized Emory up before yelling Rod's name. The audacity of this nigga to come from around the corner with a white t-shirt and pajama pants. So, this nigga got clothes and shit here too? His bitch trailed behind him. I can't even describe the look on his face when he saw me standing there. "What's up?" he asked, trying to play it cool. Like I'm not his girlfriend standing at the door while he's at another bitch's house.

"What's up? What the fuck you mean nigga?" Emory said with a disgusted look on her face.

He laughed, "Yo, Em. Check yourself." Emory backed down.

"Who are they, Roddy?" The Teana girl asked, handing him a coat.

"Roddy?" I finally spoke. "Is this how we do Rod? You're over here laid up with some bitch after you just left my fucking house?" The door girl eased back into the house.

"Bitch? I got your bitch," Teana said trying to break bad. "Rod, you better control your motherfucking groupies. This bitch got me fucked up, I keep telling you to be honest with her lame ass." She rolled her neck.

"Yo, chill out with that shit. You not gone put your hands on her T," he said to Teana. "Si, I'll call you later."

I smirked, "No, don't call me." Talk about being completely flabbergasted. I can throw up, that's how sick to my stomach I am with Rod. He was so calm and nonchalant about the situation. It's starting to feel like every month, shit every week, it's something with him. I go from madly in love to almost hating everything about him. We locked eyes when his bitch was rambling. I was seconds from hitting somebody and crying at the same time. Why am I standing on this girl's stoop checking for my man? Why do I want him to hug me and tell me he's sorry for hurting me like this again? Daddy used to always say, 'Find a man that'll never make you cry more than he makes you smile.' Well, Rod isn't that guy. I fought back the tears I wanted to shed from the hurt and this shit hurts. Just the thought of him kissing, caressing, and sexing her invades my mind. Do I need an explanation? No, I know it is exactly what it looks like. But my heart still wants him to fight for me and show some type of affection towards me to let this bitch know who has his heart. I'm out here looking stupid as hell. Times like this, I need both of my parents. Daddy to give me the caring, but tough and realistic advice. Mommy to hug me and tell me everything will be alright, even though I know it won't. I grasped Emory's hand tightly and she led me away from the cheater. She made sure I was okay to drive. With not much time remaining, I went home to get ready to take my exam. So much on my mind, I hope I can focus long enough to pass this test.

I stopped at the diner to get breakfast for Emory and me, she stayed in my bed while I went to the college to take my exam. We smoked then ate our food. I need anything to take my mind off the events that transpired this morning. I retrieved my phone from the nightstand, 110 missed calls from Rod. One sorry ass text message that read, "I'm sorry." He's damn right he's sorry, a sorry excuse of a man. This nigga thinks he can do me like that then everything is okay hours later. He really has shit twisted.

"What should I do?" I asked her.

She sighed, "I honestly can't tell you. I mean, I know what I'd do, but you have to figure it out on your own. I've been through it all with Chris, my old best friend used to tell me to do this or that, but at the end of the day, I did what Emory wanted. You're gonna have to do what you want. I'm here regardless and I'll never judge you for any decision you'll make."

The love I have for Rod is not enough to deal with the cheating and lying. It's time for me to get over him and live my life without him in it. Explore New Bern for what it is. He doesn't give a fuck about me or my feelings.

CHAPTER 10

I blocked Rod's calls from my phone. This has been a week of hell without seeing or talking to him. I've been filling my time with Emory and smoking all week. I've completed all my Christmas shopping for my family so I'm just counting the days until then.

"Nick wants us to come to his house to smoke, are you up to it?" Emory asked. We were lounging in my room fully dressed and with no plans.

"Erica's Nick?"

"He's definitely not hers, but yes, he's the one I'm talking about. We smoke together from time to time. He's just having a few of his friends over and invited us."

I made a face, "I don't know Em, how many niggas are we talking about?"

"I'm not sure, but we won't be the only females there if that's what you're worried about. Nick's girl and her clique will be over there too. I just want to smoke, for free. He supposedly has the best in town aside from our exes."

I agreed to go with her. Nick's apartment was on the front side of The Bricks. We walked in looking better than any of the other bitches in there. Of course, eyes were on us. No one looked familiar to me. People were all over the half-furnished apartment, some were smoking, kissing, and grinding to the loud music that played over the two large speakers against the wall by the stairway. I followed Emory to the small kitchen where a guy with golden dreadlocks sat on a washing machine who she informed me was Nick. She introduced us.

"What's up cuz?" He greeted Emory with a hug.

"We're here, what's good?" He slid a small bag of weed into her coat pocket.

"Your boy is about to come through. My bedroom is yours if you don't want to run into that nigga."

"Naw, it's cool, thanks for looking out." We found a spot on the only couch in the living room. This is not my kind of scene, but I'll go with the flow. I don't want to rain on anyone's parade. We prepared our mango flavored blunt with the weed she'd gotten from him. Being high makes me giggle, a lot. Everything is hilarious to me when I smoke. Blunts were being passed around the room, and we were lifted. "Turn up the music," Emory yelled. I don't know who did, but the music grew louder than it was before. She immediately started to dance in the center of the room, "Siah, come on," I joined her. We danced and laughed, the attention of everyone was invigorating. Chris walked into the apartment, he looked at us, shook his head then did whatever business he had with Nick before leaving. Emory did not seem fazed by his presence at all. I enjoy the time I spend with her, she is so full of life. I wish I could be more like her, carefree and unbothered. I sat down when she started slow grinding one of Nick's friends. Some random nigga sat beside me trying to have a conversation, but I wasn't hearing a word he was saying. Not that I wasn't interested, he was cute. I'm just too high to focus on the words coming from his mouth. My phone buzzed with a text message, Rod. I cleared the message without looking at it. Emory returned to the couch, sitting between the guy and me. "I want some dick," she whispered to me. "Should I call Chris?" I shrugged my shoulders and nodded at the same time. Better to have old dick than new, unexplored dick. Go with what you know to keep that number low. She pulled out her phone to call him, she said something then hung up. "He wants us to come to his house," she said to me.

"*Us*?" I spoke. For what? I thought. I'm not the one wanting to fuck him, besides I don't want to see Rod's lying ass.

"He said to bring you too. Maybe he wants you to watch," she laughed, but I tried to find the humor. I could just imagine the type of shit they are into. "I'll feel more comfortable if you were with me."

I reluctantly agreed because she is my friend. Although, I don't feel comfortable going to their house. Chris met us at the door inviting us into the warm house. We fled to the den. I sat in the recliner as they sat in the loveseat. "Where is everybody?" She asked for my sake rather than hers.

"Crosstown," Rod's cologne was in the air, so I knew he wasn't telling the truth. I didn't protest, I'm here for Emory.

"Let's go," she said to him. "Are you good?" She asked me. I nodded. Chris passed me the remote and they disappeared down the hall. I closed the door behind them when I got up to help myself to a shot of rum. One-shot turned into the whole damn bottle. I removed my coat, throwing it on the back of the recliner. I turned on the first movie I found before drifting off to sleep. When I awoke, I wasn't in the den, but in Rod's bed with only my bra and panties on. It was completely dark in the room. I panicked.

"Chill," he said. I covered my body with his covers. He sat at the foot of the bed.

"Where are my fucking clothes?" I questioned.

"On the floor."

"We didn't?"

"Naw, but I could've. You were whispering freaky shit in my ear, you wanted to." I'm so embarrassed. I must have blacked out. "For some reason, you took off your clothes in the den and fell asleep on the couch. I brought you in here."

"Where's Emory?"

"With Chris, why?"

"Look, whatever I said, I didn't mean." I glanced out the window, it was dark.

"Can we talk?"

I sighed loudly, "No," I picked up my clothes from the floor. "Can you take me home?"

"No," he took the clothes from my hand. I looked at him like the stupid, lying ass man he is. "Whatever you thought you saw that night was not what it seemed yo."

I laughed, "You mean to tell me, kissing and touching on that girl was not what it seems?"

"Yeah, everybody has a role to play."

"What the fuck is that supposed to mean?" I said loudly.

"Si, I have an image to uphold. Sometimes flirting with bitches is just a part of the business."

"Seems like you do more than flirt," I put my clothes on. I searched the bed for my phone.

"You don't think that I knew you were following me?"

"Well if you did and that's the decision you made then you are just as dumb as I thought. Plus, that bitch is the same bitch that claims to be your baby's mother. You're fucking these bitches then turn around to fuck me with the same dirty dick you stuck in them hoes."

He rushed towards me, "I'm not fucking anybody else," I jumped back. His eyes were lit. "And I've told you, nobody is pregnant by me."

"Whatever, you are," I said sternly, "but that's not my problem anymore keep fucking those hoes until your dick falls off. I'm over you."

"Over me?" He became aggressively upset.

"Yep, I know a couple of niggas that'll love to have me with them right now." I rolled my neck adding effect.

"Hmph," he grabbed me, tossing me on the bed. I landed hard on my stomach. The force scared me. "A couple of niggas, right?" He repeated. I stood as quickly as I could. He rushed towards me, but I pushed him back hard.

"Yeah," I challenged him. "Matter of fact, I'm late to meet a potential," I lied. I slid my arms into my coat. Rod grabbed the hood, slamming me against the wall. I yelped out, but this nigga was not about to get the best of me. I slapped him, but he only pushed me back harder.

"Don't EVER bring up another nigga around me," he clutched my face.

"FUCK YOU!" I spat. I started wailing on him. Three blows connected with his face. He has me fucked all the way up.

He grabbed my throat throwing me onto the bed again. "Watch how the fuck you talk to me," he applied enough pressure to where I couldn't breathe for a split second. I managed to knee him in the crotch which caused him to hit the floor he folded over holding his jewels.

I caught my breath as he winced from the pain, "You want me to respect you, but you don't even respect me," I knocked the things on his nightstand onto the floor. I stepped over it, "Fucking all these bitches. I'm looking like a pure fool by being with you." I pulled the covers from his bed, flinging them to the floor as well. I started talking to myself, "this nigga really got me fucked up." I continued to throw things around his room, I don't care about any of his shit he can buy more with his drug money. I threw our framed photos at him.

"Si, you better chill," One of the frames broke when I stepped on it, but I continued with my rant. He wanted to talk so Imma talk. I picked up a piece of broken glass, I slid it across his chaise ripping the leather. "Yo, chill," he said grabbing me. I reacted quickly, I cut his forearm with the glass shard. The redness of the blood snapped me back to reality.

Shit. What the fuck Siah, I thought to myself. He grabbed his arm, the blood was dripping where he stood, I immediately dropped the shard. What have I done? I wasn't trying to kill the man. I knew I shouldn't have bought my ass to this house. He covered the new wound with his left hand. I hope I didn't hit an artery. "Can you grab me a towel?" I ran as quickly as possible to the bathroom. He applied it to the wound, but the blood didn't stop.

"Rod," I started, but I didn't know what to say. This situation has gotten completely out of hand. As I looked around the room, it was a complete mess. How did I allow myself to do this? I grabbed my phone, I just wanted to leave.

As soon as I looked at my exit Rod grabbed me, "Baby, please take me to the emergency room." I didn't want to, but I did injure him. He wrapped the towel tightly around his arm. I drove to the emergency room, I contemplated whether I wanted to get out of the car or not. Rod winced the entire way to the hospital, blood was seeping through the towel onto his shirt. I helped him get out of the car, once in the hospital, he registered himself then we were placed in a patient room awaiting the doctor.

"How did this happen?" The nurse asked him. I prayed to myself hoping he wasn't going to actually tell the truth.

He paused for what felt like a lifetime, "My girlfriend," he pointed to me, "locked her keys in her car. I tried to be superman by breaking the window. I broke the window but cut my arm in the process."

The nurse nodded as he typed something into her computer. "Next time call a locksmith," she offered her advice. "How bad is the pain on a scale of one to ten?"

"Nine," he informed her. I stayed my distance from him. I feel so horrible.

"Let's take a look," she washed her hands before putting on the blue latex gloves. She removed the towel from the wound. There was so much blood she had to clean it with a wet cloth. "Looks like you're going to need sutures. Are you allergic to anything?" Rod shook his head. "Great, I'll get the doctor right in." Rod and I sat in silence once she walked out of the room. My thoughts were all over the place, I couldn't focus on anything. How did Rod and I get to this point? Physically fighting each other, that's not what love is. Even though I was defending myself I took it way too far. Rod stared at me, his eyes and facial expression softer than before.

"Si, come here," he spoke. I went to him then instantly began to sob. My emotions finally hit me. He wrapped his uninjured arm around me. "I apologize for putting my hands on you." We shared the sweetest kiss. "We have to communicate like adults," I didn't say anything. The doctor came to stitch Rod's wound. He wrote him a script for painkillers. "Can I come in," he asked when he parked in front of my house.

"I don't think that's a good idea."

"Please," he rubbed my inner thigh.

I stared out the window. "I can't do this right now," I broke down, tears streaming down my face.

"Just talk to me."

"You cheated on me, Rod. How do you expect me to be okay with that?"

"But I didn't."

"You can't even be honest with me, just keep it hot."

"I haven't fucked anybody else, I promise."

"Then what are you doing? Because from what I saw with my own two eyes, you are fucking that girl."

He looked away from me, he sighed loudly. "I'm just getting head."

"Head?" Furious, I got out of his car. Does he not know how hard it was for me to decide to suck his dick, and he's got other bitches sucking it too? He has me swapping spit with these hoes. I don't believe it's just head, because every time I do it to him, he's practically begging me to have sex.

"You got the truth," he called after me.

"So, it's supposed to make me happy? I don't know what kind of bitches you've fucked with in the past, but I'm not with that dumb shit. We're done. You're so happy with these other bitches doing things that only *I'm* supposed to do for you, what do you need me for?" The chill of the night hit my cheek. I stood in my tracks and he approached me slowly.

"I'm not used to this shit yo. I don't mean to hurt you, I swear, but shit just happens."

"Cool, let that shit happen without me bruh. For real."

"I want you to teach me," he took my hands into his.

"Teach you what? How to be faithful to a girl you claim to love? Teach you how to not lie to me? Teach you how to be a boyfriend?"

"In a sense yeah. I want to learn how to be with you. Tell me what you like and what you want from me, tell me how I can make us right again."

"Treat me how you want to be treated. But for right now, I need some space."

"I don't want space, I want you."

I rolled my eyes at him. "Rod, just leave." I left him standing there as I entered my house. Of course, he followed. I put my shoes on the mat at my bedroom door. I'm so over this nigga. I smoked the clip from the blunt Emory and I had earlier. The cannabis invaded my lungs like a weight was lifted. Rod stared at me the entire time, shaking his head. I texted Emory letting her know I was home, she's been calling me ever since she saw Rod and I leave The Hill's house. I'll call her later to give her the details I want her to have. I love Emory, but I can't tell her all my business and I know its shit she keeps from me.

"Si," Rod called out from my bedroom's door. I ignored him. He sat on my bed, "I love you. How can I make it right?"

I chuckled. "Maybe, just maybe I'll let some niggas eat my pussy, then we will be even."

He stood quickly, "I'm out, yo."

I blocked the door, "Oh, you don't like that? You got bitches putting their mouth on your shit."

"You're being childish right now, I'm not fucking these hoes. You should be honored these bitches want to taste your pussy from my dick."

"I should be honored? What the fuck is wrong with you." How does he think this is so cool? Why do I love him like this? In the back of my mind, I'm thinking I need to make a choice. Either I'm done with him or I take him back. I don't want to see him with anybody else, so he cheated, he still loves me, right? Didn't they say love conquers all? "You want to know how to make it right, don't fucking cheat."

"I won't, I promise," he said sincerely. He hugged me tightly. I made sure not to hurt his bandaged wound. "I love you so much, those bitches don't mean shit to me." It's something about the way he says things to me, so full of truth. I love this man in a way I never thought was possible. It's toxic and I can't get enough of him. He's everything I need, and I've given him all of me. It is gonna take a while before we can have sex again. I just can't put myself in danger, who knows what those girls have. Accepting his apology is hard, but I did it. Girls in Georgia use to always tell me that I didn't understand their love for the boys they were dating and now I agree…100 percent. Until you've been in love, it's not really understood why a woman would take so much from a man. My love for Rod is deep, so fucking deep. At the end of the day, I believe we will overcome everything that gets in the way of our love. I promise, on my parents' graves.

CHAPTER 11

Christmas, my favorite holiday. The second year without our parents. I remember growing up, Daddy would give us each $75.00 each to get Mom a present for Christmas, then Mom would give us another $75.00 each to get Daddy a gift. Shae, the cheap one would combine the money getting them an inexpensive, unthoughtful gift. She would pocket the rest of the money. Kennon would do like Shae, but he would give the rest of the money back. I would get them each the gift they wanted. Mom always dropped hints and Daddy laid little clues around the house. I wasn't the perfect child, but I love my parents and they did so much for us it was the least we could do. I miss them I would do anything to hear their voices again. Rod has been a gentleman today considering the holiday without my parents. He has been catering to my every need. We spent the first half of today with my family. Kendra, Shae, and Kennon loved the gifts I got for them. I didn't get anything for Peanut, he and Kendra have been having a hard time and he's barely at the house anymore. She told us he had a baby on the way by some girl in Trenton. Are all the guys in New Bern incapable of being faithful? They'll work their own shit out, I have my own problems. Now, we are at Rod's house. We'd decided to open our gifts to each other when we manage to sneak away for some alone time. Rod and I picked out gifts for his parents last week, I can't wait to see their faces when they open it. We got his mom a charm bracelet with each of her kids' names on each charm, and his dad a personalized wallet with a picture of Mrs. Robin. They handed me a gift, I didn't expect anything from them, but I'm glad they thought of me. They'd brought me a fleece blanket with slippers to match. We thanked each other for the gifts then retreated to the dining room for dinner. Dinner was good as usual. Rod prepared majority of the meal, a family tradition they started when Rod showed the interest of being a chef. All their children had a plus one, Emory with Chris, Me with Rod, Shae with Raymond, Q had some random chick, and Erica with Nick, surprisingly. I bet Emory had something to do with that. When dinner was over, we gathered in the living room with dessert as we watched a Christmas movie, another tradition of theirs. I sat between Rod's legs on the shagged carpet. We snuggled under my new fleece. The television produced the only light in the house. Rod fondled my breast underneath the cover while he suckled on my neck. I looked to make sure eyes weren't watching us. His slick ass made his way to my pants parting my legs with his other hand, he fingered me slowly.

"Can I get in this tonight?" He breathed into my ear. I'll admit it's been hard holding out on Rod, especially when he's doing things like this. I shook my head and he continue to finger me, "Can I at least taste it?" He bit my earlobe.

"Rod, are you paying attention?" Mrs. Robin asked.

"Of course, Ma," he removed his hand then licked those fingers, "Mmm, yeah, I got to have it…tonight," he whispered. I smirked, Rod has been trying hard all week. I allow him to touch because I love being touched, but I draw the line at penetration and oral. I know he wants it bad, and to be honest, I do too. My toy has been filling some of the voids.

Erica left out returning with Drea. I wonder if there is a day that these chicks don't spend together. Drea waved at everyone in the room, everyone waved back. "Hey Ray," she said. Shae looked at me. Although it was dark, I caught the evil eye she displayed.

"What's up," he said not turning his attention to her.

"It's you?" Shae said over the t.v. She knows better. Handle your business in private. Mrs. Robin shushed her.

"Yo, let's go to the den," Rod suggested. I wanted to finish the movie. We all headed to the den, except for Mr. Quentin and Mrs. Robin. They didn't question us, I guess they wanted to finish the movie in peace. Rod closed the door behind us, I stayed close to him. What the fuck is going on? I hate secret shit. Emory sat on the arm of Chris' chair.

"This is the bitch you're fucking Ray?" Shae folded her arms.

"Who?" Raymond asked her. His siblings glared at him. I'm sure they knew the answer.

"Who?" Shae mimicked him, "This bitch," she pointed to Drea.

"Ray, you might as well tell her," Drea said. Shorty has balls.

We all waited for Raymond's response. Shae was getting furious by the seconds. "No, I'm not fucking her."

"No? Really Ray?" Drea looked hurt.

"The man said no, get off his back," Chris chimed in.

"Chris shut the fuck up," Drea fussed.

"Watch your mouth bitch," Emory said, I laughed.

"Em!" Erica exclaimed.

"Get your friend because I don't play about mine. She better ask her cousin."

"What does my cousin have to do with any of this?" Drea asked.

"I beat her ass and I'll beat you if you say another thing out the way to Chris," Emory stood with her hands on her hips. "You and Yazzy are some disrespectful ass bitches, but I'm not the one."

"Iight, Em," Chris said to her, hoping she'll back down.

"*You're* Yazzy's cousin?" I asked Drea, she nodded. Now I'm confused. When I first met these bitches, they had so much to say about Yazzy, but Drea neglected to tell me that they were related.

"The way this bitch is acting, tells me what I need to know," Shae said.

Raymond, still playing it cool. He must have learned that from Rod. "I just said I'm not fucking her, and I'm not about to have this conversation in front of everybody."

"Why not bro? We're dying to know," Q chimed in playfully.

"It's not ya'll business, this is between me and my girl."

"Bro, chill with that fuck boy shit. You fucking Drea or not?"

"No, I just said that shit. Have I fucked the bitch? Yeah, way before I got with Shae. I'm with who I want," he pulled Shae closer to him. "Drea too crazy to accept that shit and quite frankly I don't know why she's here trying to fuck up our day."

"Ray, you said we were going to always be together," Drea pouted.

"That was before I met my girl. Erica, get her the fuck out of here."

"You've been playing with my feelings for a long time. I'm not going to let him go so easily because he *thinks* he has something with this girl. How many girls has it been? They go and I'm still here?"

"Sorry hun, that's your dumbness, but I'm not going anywhere," Shae said to her. All of us were watching them like we were watching a movie. I felt for Drea, we used to hang out all the time and she's a cool ass chick. She's playing herself by stepping in this house like Raymond was going to ride off into the sunset with her. She never expressed to me that Raymond was the guy she was so in love with probably because I'm related to Shae.

"He'll come running back, he always does."

"Girl get the fuck. You hoes are only good for one thing, a quick nut," that was Emory adding in her two cents.

"Yo, Drea it's time for you to leave," Rod said opening the door for her and Erica to walk out.

"Man, roll one," Chris called out.

"Fuck that, roll two," Rod said. The four brothers each rolled a blunt while the girls talked about what just occurred. Q's little ragamuffin looked scared, she probably thinks we're crazy. We played Charades and smoked.

"Oooh, let's play truth or dare," Emory suggested.

"Hell no, Em you don't know how to behave," Q said to her.

"I swear I will," she promised. We sat coupled, "Chris go first."

"Naw, how this nigga gets to go first?" Raymond argued.

"My game, my rules," Emory proudly sang, "Go, baby."

"Truth or dare bro?" Chris asked Q.

"I'm not fucking with ya'll tonight, truth."

"Ass or toes?"

"Nigga, both. Big bro can teach you a thing or two about pleasing a woman," we all laughed.

"Siah…truth or dare sis?" Q asked.

"Um…I don't know, truth."

"Booooo," Emory said, letting me know that she didn't agree with my choice.

"Do you cum harder when it's fast or slow?" Q asked.

I looked at Rod who was anticipating my answer. I felt like this was a trick question. Should I answer? Fuck it, why not, "deep and slow," I smiled.

"Good shit bro," his brothers dapped him.

I rolled my eyes playfully, "Truth or dare, Raymond?"

"Truth."

"What's your body count?"

"Roughly sixty."

"Damn Ray," Emory exclaimed, "Damn near all the bitches in The Bricks."

"What? These niggas got way more than me."

"Damn Ray, where is the bro code at?" Rod laughed, I cut my eyes at him. The game went on, more sexual secrets were exposed as everyone chose truth. It was entertaining. Mrs. Robin brought fresh-baked gingerbread cookies with cranberry spritz to the den. She is such a sweet lady, and she didn't say anything about us smoking. Soon after the snacks were finished Shae and Raymond exited the room, then Erica and Nick, Q and his girl as well. Rod and I watched a movie with Emory and Chris.

"Bro, we're about to do a bump, you want some?" Chris asked Rod, but he shook his head. I didn't know Emory was into that until they both exited to the bathroom.

"I want some of you," Rod climbed on top of me, pushing me back on the chair arm. Our breathing changed as we locked lips. Rod removed his shirt revealing his chocolate body. I ran my hands over his abs. He lifted my shirt to remove my bra.

My eyes glanced towards the restroom, I didn't want Emory and Chris to walk in on us. "Not in here," I said to him.

He caressed my breasts, "It's okay, I'll be quick." He now sat upright on the couch, "Come here," he requested in a low tone. He slid his jeans, gym shorts, and boxers to his ankles, his harden dick sprung out. I slid out of my bottoms, he turned me around kissing my left ass cheek then sat me on his dick, I gasped. I held onto his knees as I rode his dick... *my* dick. Rod's hands tingled my spine, I looked back at Rod and his eyes were closed. He bit his bottom lips as I grinded on him. I could hear Emory's moans from the bathroom. Rod bent me over the couch he thrust inside me at a rapid pace. I rubbed my clit, I came, then he came. His cum invading my pussy. We collapsed on the couch out of breath. I've missed this.

Chris and Emory walked out of the bathroom. They both laughed when they saw Rod and I trying to cover our bodies. Emory held her hands over both of their eyes as they made their way out of the den. Rod and I dressed then went to his room. I lay on his warm bed exhausted from the long day and the sex. Rod towered over me kissing my neck then my chest. "Have I told you how much I love you?" He kissed me, I held onto his face. "I know I've fucked up, and that'll never happen again. I don't want to put you into a predicament where you can't trust me," he stared into my eyes. "Promise me one thing, you'll never leave me," I saw his eyes began to glisten with forming tears. I'm not sure where this was coming from, but I adore his vulnerable side.

I pulled him close, kissing him, "I'll never leave you." Rod hugged me snugly, moments like this solidifies why I fell in love with him. Under his tough exterior and the image he has to uphold is a man that loves the hell out of me. We embraced; Rod went to his closet to retrieve a black, small velvet box. When he handed it to me, I opened it carefully. I love him, but it is way too soon for a marriage proposal. I don't even know if marriage is on the table for us. The box revealed a black diamond ring. Three black prongs separated each stone, it was so beautiful. My suspicion was subsided when he took the ring from the box to place it on my right ring finger.

"A promise ring and I promise to give you all of me, no bullshit. No other bitches, just us and nobody will come between our bond." He wiped my happy tears, then kissed me, "Also," he pulled a different gift box from his dresser. He opened it and, two keys hung from the single key ring. I was a little confused, it didn't look like a car key, "I got us an apartment in Winchester," I was beyond flattered. What will my sisters and brother think? I don't even know if I'm ready for this. "When I first met you, I knew we'd be together for the long haul. I've never felt the way I feel about you with another girl. I want us to continue to grow with each other that's why I want us to move in together."

"Of course, I'll move in with you," I said a little too happily, but I was thrilled. I've been thinking about getting my own place, but I also loved having all my siblings together in one home, we haven't had that in a long time. The way I'm feeling right now is probably how someone feels once they find out they've won the lottery. Excited but also worried about what others would think. I'm ready to see what our future holds, I finally got a man! I retrieved the gifts I got for Rod from the corner. I got him a game system with games, I know I will grow to regret the decision of giving him a gaming system, so I got myself a controller and headset as well.

He thanked me with more kisses. I giggled. "Once we move in together, you *have* to be a part of my world. That does mean every aspect of me and my current way of getting money," he waited for my answer or rather my agreeance.

I thought for a minute before responding to him, "I'm with it."

I found love. My mom and dad had that special love, they were perfect. They never argued or disagreed in front of us. They laughed and smiled more than anyone I've ever known. The way my parents looked at each other was magical. My dad never raised his voice at my mom, he talked to her with the utmost respect. My mom never belittled Daddy or undermined him. They were a team and if you were against one, you went against both. They complimented each other all the time, they just loved each other to the core, and I think I found a love like theirs. Daddy would bring Mom flowers every Friday, it was their ritual. They showered us and each other with gifts, but it wasn't only about the gifts and what they could do for one another, their bond was much deeper than that. Total strangers could walk into our home and feel the love in the air. I want that for the home Rod and I will soon share because the bond Rod and I have is profound.

CHAPTER 12

It's been so hard trying to get our apartment how I want it. When we moved out, we decided to purchase new things. Everything in our apartment we picked out together. I convinced him in buying a giraffe print sectional for the living room as well as giraffe print king sized bed set. To say the least everything in our apartment has the giraffe print and each room is themed giraffe. It's like walking into an African savanna. I couldn't enjoy New Year's Day because of all the shit I had to do. I'm so glad I decided to sit out of school this semester. With all of what I have going on, my schoolwork would have suffered. I talked to Rod about it and he supported my decision. Rod's birthday is today, and I've planned a surprise party in our new home. I've been running around all day like a chicken with its head cut clean off. I'm so thankful for Emory, baby girl has been so helpful to me. She picked up his cake from the bakery, the food and my outfit. With the apartment in good standing, I decorated with colorful lights. I've invited everyone, except Yazzy. I don't want her anywhere near me or Rod. I told all the guests to arrive at 7:30 p.m. and did 7:30 p.m. come fast. I dressed in my new blue Bohemian style floral dress. Dimanasia braided my hair in long, single braids and now I feel like Rapunzel with the hair flowing down my back.

"Surprise!" Everyone yelled when Rod walked into our apartment.

He was smiling so hard, I kissed him, "Happy Birthday Baby," I whispered in his ear. He kissed me back thanking me. I motioned for the deejay also known as Chris to turn the music up. I watched as Rod walked around the apartment greeting friends and family. This is the happiest I've seen him. Everyone danced and vibed to the music, Emory handed me a cup of her specialty mixed drink. She wouldn't share the recipe with me, but it is delicious, and the taste of liquor isn't there. Of course, everyone was smoking as well, I've allowed it for the first time in this apartment because it's a special occasion. I excused myself to the bathroom, I've been running to the bathroom since I've started drinking. Rod was in the doorway as I finished up.

"I gotta make a run," he pulled me into his arms, he began to lift my dress caressing my bare buttocks.

"Right now?" I hope from my tone he understands that now wasn't a good time. He covered my mouth with his. Rod is always trying to butter me up with his sex appeal.

"It'll only take a second," he lifted me onto the vanity. He suckled on my neck.

It took me a minute to escape the trance he'd put me in, "No," I pouted, I pushed him back playfully. I'm not about to explain to a room full of people why the man of the hour isn't here.

He adjusted his hardening dick, "I wasn't asking. I gotta make this money."

"Whatever, Rod," I mumbled as he left out. It's all about money to him as of late. Money can wait at least until the party for *him* is over. I love money, but not as much as I love my life and the people in it. I'm starting to think this apartment must have put a damper on how much money he can save. He pays the rent, light bill and buys the food for the house, I pay for the internet and any necessities we need. Rod also gives me money daily I don't even have to touch my bank account unless I want to. My baby spoils me, but I rather have *him* over anything. I don't need his money. I went back to the party guests. I wanted to pout the entire time he was gone, but I didn't want to ruin the party for everyone else plus the liquor was making it impossible to not have a good time. Rod came back within thirty minutes of him leaving, I lit up when he stepped back into our home. The specialty drink had me feeling amazing. I grabbed him, leading him to the middle of the living room. After a couple of dances with him, I retrieved the cookies and cream cake with the candled numbers '2' and '9'. We sang our version of the Happy Birthday song then Rod blew out the candles. We shared a piece of cake, he dipped his finger in the icing. I licked the icing from his fingertips. I want him to know that when these guests leave…it's on. The guests left before midnight, I cleaned while Rod showered. I patted myself on the back for throwing my man this awesome party. I crept to our bedroom, I wanted to shower before I gave Rod his pussy. I was taken aback when I approached the cracked door and heard a female's voice on his speaker. He has a lot of nerve, I thought to myself.

"Damn, I couldn't get an invite to your birthday party?" She laughed and my anger grew.

"Chill, yo. You know that can't happen, niggas ain't fucking with you right now."

"I got something for you though."

"What's that?"

"You're gonna have to wait until you come over, that is if you can get away."

He chuckled that sly laugh I love, and thought was only meant for me. Who is this bitch? "Are you gonna be at Yazzy's spot later?"

I burst into the room, attitude on ten thousand. "Who the fuck is you talking to Rod?" I grabbed the phone out his hand, "Who the fuck is this?"

The bitch on the other end laughed, "This Lauryn."

"Are you fucking him?"

"Si, give me my fucking phone, yo," he said calmly, nothing ruffles his feathers and that annoys me.

I gave him a look of disgust, "Fuck you. Now answer my question, bitch."

"Bro ain't my type," she laughed. "I see ya'll have shit to discuss. Tell Rod to call me later." *Call disconnected.*

Tossing the phone beside him I retrieved my suitcase from the closet, I threw half of my clothes in it. We are going down the same road again. He promised to never put me through this shit again. Does this promise mean nothing to him?

He watched as I ran around the room like a madwoman. "Where are you going?"

"Back home, and I'm done with your cheating, lying ass."

He sighed heavily, "Here we go again, I'm not cheating, and what am I lying about?"

"Who is Lauryn?"

"Best friend."

"Best friend?" I scoffed as I slammed the suitcase shut.

"Yo, you're always jumping to conclusions and I hate that shit."

I stood with my hands on my hips, "And you're always fucking other bitches. That shit is lame as fuck. Grow the fuck up!"

"Watch your mouth," he glared at me with seriousness.

"Or what?" I challenged him.

He stood, "Nothing yo, I'm done with you. You can leave."

I froze, I couldn't believe what just came from his mouth, "What?" My voice trembled.

"You heard me loud and clear. I'm not about to deal with a bitch that thinks she's right when she's wrong."

"Well stop giving me reasons."

"I'm not giving you reasons, you're looking for shit. I had the bitch on speaker. If I had anything to fucking hide, I would've stepped the fuck out to make the call. Think sometimes instead of assuming shit. Now that shit is lame. So, continue to pack, make sure you pack all your shit, you got to go." After all the shit I've done for him today and he disrespects me like this? I've never seen him this angry before and it's scary. I headed towards the front door with tears in my eyes. "And know that when you walk out that door, you're not coming back and lose my fucking number."

I turned back to him, "What do you want from me?"

"I want you to fucking trust me. FUCK! Is that too much to ask? I can't...I won't be in a relationship like this yo. I got too many bitches on my dick to be sitting here putting up with your insecurities." I sat on the couch feeling defeated. I've turned into a paranoid bitch. I fought back the tears so hard that my eyes were beginning to hurt.

"What's it gonna be? Are you gonna start trusting me or what?" I nodded, "Naw yo, I need you to speak up."

"Yes," I looked at him, "I'll start trusting you," he walked back to our bedroom closing the door behind him. I cried myself to sleep on the couch on his birthday night.

The next morning Rod slammed a package down on the coffee table, I immediately woke from my slumber. The familiar clear wrapping around the package gave away what it was. I rubbed my swollen eyes, Rod was standing over me. "It's time to prove your loyalty yo."

"What do you want me to do?" I sat up to find my back was feeling the uncomfortable effects of the couch.

"Deliver this brick to my boy in Morehead City," he said nonchalantly. He was so cool and casual with his request like what he was asking of me wasn't insane. "I'll text you the address after you go pick up Lauryn."

"What?! Are you out of your mind? I'm not taking this shit with a bitch I don't know." He's forcing me to hang around this bitch.

"Baby," he pulled me from the couch and wrapped his arms around my waist. He kissed me with the same lips that disrespected me last night. Staring into his eyes makes me overlook the hurtful words he said. "I need you to do this for me. I've never asked a female I've been dealing with to move weight for me, but I want to show you how much I trust you, so you can learn to trust me. I know you can do this."

"Give me the details."

"Make the delivery and he'll give you the bread. Simple shit."

"And where are you gonna be?"

"I have to go handle somebody," Rod and I made up from last night. I got dressed then headed on my way. I thought I was going to be delivering one brick, but he handed me an overnight bag with two bricks in it. I tossed the bag in the trunk of my car. I thought about what my dad would say if he saw me right now. I pushed the disappointment I know he would feel in the back of my mind. My palms are sweaty, and I can't focus. My mind is racing from getting caught by the police, to having to deal with a chick that may be fucking my boyfriend, to driving this shit all the way to Morehead. Plus, I don't know this guy what if he kills me and takes the drugs? Rod told me to pick Lauryn up from Yazzy's house. I blew my horn for her, you won't find me knocking on that dirty ass door. A girl with lemonade braids, a peacoat and skin-tight pants came to my car. She's dark-skinned with full lips and her eyes are big and brown.

"Hey!" She said putting her seatbelt on, "I'm Lauryn, remember we talked for a little bit last night?" She snickered.

"Siah," I glared at her. So, this is his "best friend"? Why am I just now meeting this "best friend"?

"It's nice to finally meet you," she laughed.

She was irritating me, and it hasn't been five minutes yet, "Look, all that snarky ass laughing is rather annoying. I'm trying to find the humor. Rod wants you here, not me. Try not to irritate me while going to Morehead or I'll put your ass out my car and have you walking back to this dirty ass house," I said matter-of-factly. I tapped into my inner Emory.

She nodded, "You got it." I entered the address Rod texted into my phone's navigation app. Since Rod wants me to be ride or die, I will be that and more. I made sure the music was blasting in the car, I don't care about her and I don't want to make small talk. She is irrelevant to me. I parked in front of a two-story mint green beach house. I grabbed the bag from the trunk then proceeded to the door with Lauryn in tow.

The door flung open before I could even knock. A heavy-set white guy stood at the door looking meaner than mean. "Password," was all he spoke then glared at us.

Confusion took over my entire body. Password? I thought to myself. When did Rod give me a password? Was I not listening? I'm standing here with a bag full of illegal drugs and no password to enter. Sweat beads formed and dripped alongside my face. I looked around to access the area, I may have to make a run for it. Do I drop the bag then run? Or do I haul ass with the drugs? What if he shoots me in the back? I'll be all over the news, 'Drug dealing LaSiah

Martin' gunned down amidst a drug exchange. Fuck me! I began to back away, I don't have the answer, Rod can do this shit himself.

"The password is Si," Lauryn said as I bumped into her. The bodyguard stepped aside, we entered the empty beach house. No furniture, no pictures, no carpet. Just a couple of lawn chairs and a kitchen table.

"Take a seat," said a light-skinned guy that was sitting at the kitchen table. He looked familiar but, the one thing that stood out was the way he dressed given the environment and the nature of this exchange. He had on a tailored business suit. This guy takes his business serious. Lauryn and I sat. "Which one is Si?" I raised my hand like I was in school. "Let me see it," I unzipped the bag on the table so he could see the product, but he didn't look at it. "Two keys, right?"

"Yeah, sure," I nodded with uncertainty.

"Grab that bag over there," he pointed towards a bag in the corner. I followed his directions, retrieved the bag, throwing the strap onto my shoulder. It was heavy. I sat it beside the bag from Rod, the guy unzipped it revealing a shit ton of money bundled together. I did it, my work is done. I can't wait to get home: Mission Complete. "Always count your shit, we got time." He requested a money counter from the bodyguard, "Give us a minute," Lauryn and the bodyguard cleared the room. Why would her dumb ass leave me alone with him? I know we got off on the wrong foot, but damn. I would never just leave a female alone with someone she doesn't know and clearly isn't comfortable with. I sat in a nearby chair as I ran the bundles through the machine. He watched closely.

"This is over $50,000," I stated. I was beyond shocked and flattered at the same time, Rod trusts me with this much money.

"And an extra $2,000, let Rod know it is for handling that shit with Daniel, I appreciate that."

I put the money back into the bag, "We're done right? Hopefully, you don't have to see me again because this type of work isn't for me."

"Yeah, you're good. I'd never let my girl move weight for me, but I can teach you some things though on some real shit," he flirted.

"Cause when you lay with niggas like me and Rod, it's no telling who or what you'll have to deal with."

"I'm starting to realize that, but I'm learning not to complain or ask questions. The less I know, the better."

"Naw, you gotta know. Educate yourself on this business, especially if you and Rod are going to be together long term. A lot of trust has been placed in you. Trust me when I say this, niggas come themselves when that much money in is play. My boy Rod has a soft spot for you." I smiled. In the back of my mind, I wish that were true. As many bitches as I was last night, I'm guessing somewhere in that soft spot is also a hard stone. I didn't ask the guy for his name nor did he offer it, in a way that's better. He called his bodyguard and Lauryn back into the room, I forgot I was with that bitch.

"Let's go," I said brushing past her and out the beach house.

After several minutes of silence, Lauryn started to grill me, "What did he say?"

"Nothing," I lied shrugging her off. For one, I don't know this hoe, and two, it's none of her damn business. If he wanted her to know he would have kept her hoe ass in the room.

"Rod's not gonna like the fact ole boy wanted to be alone with you."

"Let me worry about Rod and you worry about yourself," I spat. At this point, I don't give a fuck what Rod likes and doesn't like. He should have gone himself. I handed the bag to Rod as soon as I got home, I brought Lauryn with me upon his request. I'm so glad that is over with. I grabbed bottled water before joining him on the couch.

"Thanks, Baby," Rod said. He looked as if he was having a bad day. We shared a quick kiss. "What's good, Lauryn?" He dabbed her like he does his boys. I'm not a fan of this relationship, but we will see how this plays out. "How did it go?" He asked her more than me.

"Ask your girl, she handled everything. Zo sent me and his shadow out of the room. He wanted a private meeting with her," I can't believe the nerve of this bitch. She's making it sound way worse than it was. I could hear the jealousy in her voice.

Rod looked at me confused, "Private meeting? What did he say?"

"He had me count the money, then thanked you with extra for the Daniel situation," I rolled my eyes at Lauryn, petty bitch.

"So, it's all there?" I nodded. Rod gave Lauryn a grand then sent her on her way. I'm not sure why because she didn't do anything. "Sí?" he called me into the bedroom. I leaned against the door frame, "Thank you for handling that business today. I know it wasn't easy for you to do." He smiled at me and at that moment, I felt proud of myself. I helped my man out with something never trusted from any of the thots he's dealt with in the past. He pressed me gently against the wall, "Have you ever made love on a bed full of money?" He said seductively in my ear. I shook my head. He emptied all the money onto our bed. A wide grin spread across his face and we made love on the money. "You're never getting rid of me," Rod whispered.

"I wouldn't dream of it," I kissed his neck.

CHAPTER 13

Rod and I have officially declared today, Rod and LaSiah Day. He's cooked breakfast and lunch. For dinner we ordered Chinese take-out. We have been chilling in our bed all day long in our pajamas. Phones turned down, just enjoying each other with no interruptions, except going to the bathroom. Rod and I need a day like this. He rubbed my belly because it was aching from eating too much. He attempted to go lower, but I put a halt to that because I just wanted his company besides, we can do the nasty things another time. We got through two more movies before his phone started to buzz.

He grabbed his phone from the coffee table, looking at it he said, "I'll be back babe."

"Why? Can't Chris or Ray do your runs today?" I pouted.

He stood, gathering his shoes and coat, "No, not for these clients."

"Babe, please?" I whined.

"I'll be right back," he left. I was furious. I checked my phone to find a text from Dimanasia inviting Shae and I to a sexy pajama party tonight. Even though she was last minute with the invitation I confirmed my attendance. I guess I can use a little fun and since Rod has decided to abandon our date day this party has come at the right time. I know this party is going to be the most ratchet, but entertaining party I've ever been to. I found a comfortable pajama set, a blue long-sleeved shirt that displayed more cleavage than usual and striped plush pajama pants. I think Aaron may have brought this set for me one Christmas or birthday. I didn't want to be too sexy because it's no telling who Dimanasia has invited to this party. Spraying on my favorite perfume was the finishing touches to my appearance. Rod's always skipping out on me so now it's my time to skip out on him. I texted him before I walked into Dimanasia's decked out apartment. Girls were everywhere, all shapes and sizes. It was around twelve of us.

"Okay ladies, gather around," she announced once she noticed me. We sat on her multicolored rug in her living room, "Welcome to my lingerie party! Thank you all for coming. Tonight, we are going to enjoy ourselves, I have a bunch of games for us to play, food to eat and toys that will blow your mind. Let your hair down and remember; what happens here..." She paused awaiting our answer.

"Stays here," we responded in unison. Emory walked in dressed in a plush buffalo plaid pajama set. She is so cute. I ran over to her because I was so happy to see a familiar face. I don't know Dimanasia's friends and Shae hasn't shown up yet.

I haven't seen or talked to Emory since Rod's party a couple of days ago. I wanted to tell her about the drug deal Rod had me go on, but then again maybe that's not the best idea. I don't want people knowing that I, LaSiah Martin is a drug dealer even if it was one time. "About time," I said to her. I texted her as soon as I decided to come out.

"Sorry babe, Chris was trippin'. How did you get out?"

"Well he ditched me to make a run, so I texted him letting him know I was stepping out."

"Bitch! He's gonna get your ass," we laughed.

"Not if I find something here that we can both enjoy."

"Yuck, don't make me puke," I pushed her playfully. We walked around looking at the various sizes of dildos and vibrators. Smirking like we were little girls. Dimanasia's apartment was decked out. She made space for two rectangle tables to be placed in the living room, the room was dim and most of everything was decorated in yellow. Different samples of sexual products graced the tables and there were order forms in case we wanted something Dimanasia did not have in stock. She even had a mannequin dressed in lingerie, another item she had for sale. I was tempted to purchase one until I found the price tag, too steep for me. Nakedness will have to do. All the women chatted amongst themselves as they looked through the inventory. We played Dimanasia's freaky games like, pin the dick on the man, how fast can you suck with a baby's bottle. Shae walked into the apartment towards the end of the party, the part when Dimanasia was handing all the ladies small gifts bags as a token for participating at her party. I was feeling good from the all the shots Dimanasia had us take every hour, on the hour. I can say, cuz threw a really good party. I did purchase a couple of items to support her, massaging oil, penis candies and Emory made me buy a big, black dildo just because she got one.

All the party guests cleared out of the apartment, Shae, Emory, and I stayed to help Dimanasia clean up. "My dude having a party in Havelock. We should go turn up," Dimanasia said as she stood over a bag of trash.

"They got bud?" Emory asked. Not surprised at all, this girl loves smoking and getting high and it is a plus if it's free.

"Yes, of course," Dimanasia answered.

"Let's ride then," Emory ran to the door. I was skeptical, plus Rod hasn't even texted me back. "Bring ya ass, Siah."

"Pause, do you see what the fuck we have on?" I folded my arms against my chest.

"So, bitch, we're fly as fuck," Shae chimed in, I looked at her wearing a burgundy onesie. "I mean seriously Siah, have you even seen how some girls go to a party up here? Trust me, our attire is more than fine."

I agreed to go with the girls against my better judgment. Dimanasia drove to a small building on the back roads of Havelock. The party was packed as fuck and Shae was right, we were not the worst dressed at the party, but we did stand out. We drunk, we danced, we smoked with random people, we were just all around lit. Dimanasia dipped off with 'her dude'. While Shae and Emory kept dancing, I found me a spot at the bar.

"Is this not your scene?" The bartender leaned over to ask me. I looked back at him and he didn't strike me as a bartender. Maybe he was only making sure niggas didn't drink all the alcohol. He was a beautiful man, tall, light-skinned with curly hair. He looked out of place. His smile faded when I didn't answer his question fast enough, maybe I was too busy admiring his features. "Are you okay? Do you need a water?"

"Oh yeah, I mean no…. I mean." I stopped to gather my words, he had me flustered. "I'll take rum," he poured my glass, our hands touched as I reached for the glass. I allowed his fingertips to linger on mine, they were soft, and the touch was electric.

"So, what's your name?" He tried to say over the music, the song changed but I could barely hear him.

"I can't hear you," I said to him while gesturing to my ears. He motioned for me to come behind the bar. It still wasn't 100% quieter back there because the speaker was so close, but I was closer to him. I must admit he intrigues me.

"I asked for your name," he leaned in again to say to me.

"Tell me yours first."

He passed a beer to someone, "Xavier."

"Are you from around here?" I asked him.

"I'm from Harlowe, are you going to ignore my question?" He handed out another beer. I've heard of Harlowe, but I don't know exactly where it is. All I know is that it's somewhere past Havelock.

"I'm LaSiah," he placed his hand on the small of my back as he handed out yet another beer. Amidst all the sweat, musk and ass in the air, he smelt good. I poured myself another shot of rum and consumed it quickly. I know I looked awkward being behind this bar chopping it up with this tall glass of caramel milk. "Is this like your job?"

"No, I'm helping out my friend."

"That's nice of you."

"It comes with its benefits like talking with beautiful girls," I smiled. My eyes diverted from him to an altercation happening across the room. One dude started to push another, somebody shouted something about a gun then all hell broke loose. The crowd rushed to the exit doors all at once. I panicked, I tried to search the room for Shae, Emory and Dimanasia but I didn't see any of them. Xavier took my hand guiding through the back exit.

"Wait, I have to find my girls," I could not leave them in this club.

"It's not safe to go back in there, try to call them."

Good idea I thought. I called Shae and she let me know that she was with Emory and they were in front of the club. I walked to the front with Xavier in tow. It was like a fight scene out of movies when we approached the front. Almost everyone was fighting. Emory was recording it all. Dimanasia was standing with them. The cops pulled up and that was everybody's cue to scatter. Xavier walked with us to Dimanasia's car. They nudged and snickered with each other, but they didn't say anything about Xavier.

"Can I have your number? Or is this like a once in a lifetime thing?"

I smiled as I held my hand out for his phone, "make sure you use it," I typed my name and number then handed it back to him. He could turn out to be a great friend. I climbed in Dimanasia's car. We got back to her house before 1 a.m.

"We have to do this again," Dimanasia laughed.

"I don't know, Ray's been blowing my shit up," Shae said as she retreated to her car.

I'm salty because Rod hasn't called or texted me. I hate when he doesn't check on me. I feel like he doesn't give a fuck. I walked into our apartment to find him in the living room asleep on the couch. I rubbed his beautiful face to awake him.

"Damn, hey Baby, where have you been?" He sat up rubbing his red eyes.

"My cousin had a party, then we went to another party. Did you get my text?"

"Naw," I noticed the drugs and money on the coffee table. This is what had him tied up. His first love, money is more important than me. "You went to a party dressed like that?"

I laughed, "It's a long story, want to join me in the shower?"

"Naw, I'm good. I gotta pack this shit up."

I rolled my eyes. I grabbed a pint of ice cream from the kitchen then sat down beside Rod. "You need help?"

He smirked, "No, Si." He appeared to be annoyed. He always gets like this when he's high off coke. He started to weigh and package the pack.

"Why do you use?" I played with the ice cream with the spoon. I've always wondered, but I never had the courage to ask him.

He glared at me, and I put my head down. "I stand behind my shit, for one. And two, I need the right kind of high sometimes."

"How is it different from getting high when you smoke weed?"

"Think of it like this, with weed I'm laid back. With coke, it puts me in a party mode, it's like a rush."

"Can I try it?" I sat the pint of ice cream on the coffee table and waited for his answer.

After about two minutes of silence he spoke, "No," he said sternly. "I don't ever want you touching this shit. I never wanted you around it."

"Why?" I challenged. I'm not sure if I really wanted to try coke or if I wanted to know what his reaction would be. This high he explained seems like it would be dope. I need a rush to get shit off my mind, the shit I don't want to think about anymore.

"Because I said so," he cleared the table of the small packages he'd already made. Tossing them into the nearby backpack.

"That's not fair though. It's cool and okay if you do it, but I can't. I'm not a child Rod. Either I try it with you, or I'll find somebody else who'll give it to me."

He sucked his teeth because he knows coke isn't hard to find in this town. Rod retrieved a small packet from his jeans, "You're not getting a lot, just enough for you to feel it." My heart started to pound in my ears as he pulled out a small case from the side of the sofa. It contained an empty glass vial with a tiny ass spoon inside. He scooped the spoon into the cocaine packet then held it to my face, "here, sniff it deep, but not too hard," he instructed.

"The whole thing?" I asked looking at the amount. It sure seemed like awfully a lot.

"Yeah, the whole thing. Do you want me to show you?" I nodded. I watched as he held his right nostril then snorted the cocaine into the left. It was so quick, and he made it look easy. He held his head back for a hot minute. He rubbed his nose then smiled at me. He dipped the spoon into the packet again and offered it to me again. This time when he held it to my face, I mimicked his previous actions. It almost felt like a brain freeze, but as I threw my head back it subsided. All I felt was an instant rush, and I felt like I could fly right out of this apartment. We stared at each other for about three minutes. A burst of energy came over me. I have never felt this good before, so untouchable. It felt like I've drank twenty cans of an energy drink. Rod touched my arm and it felt like his skin was one-thousand degrees. "You feel that shit, Baby?" I nodded. I was for sure having an out of body experience, and I was enjoying it. I turned on our music player, I wanted to dance.

"Dance with me," I said alluring him.

He licked his juicy lips, "Naw, dance for me," I turned to my favorite song then I stripped for him. I peeled every article of clothing off. I felt so alive. Rod's seductive eyes were eying my every move. He'd even slid out of his own clothing. "Come here," he beckons for me. We made love so intensely like our lives depended upon it. We folded into each other's arms. The sun started to peak through the shades. Our high was coming down. "So, what do you think?" He asked. Our naked, sweaty bodies clung to one another.

"It was cool, but I'll have to do that when I go out with my girls because that energy was too high. I literally tried to fuck your brains out."

"Yeah, I know, that shit was good as hell. On a serious note, I don't want you on that shit yo'. Emory already be geeking off that shit."

"I'm not her, and that feeling it just gave me was amazing. I'd like to try it again." Who am I? Did I just admit that I like doing cocaine? I mean, movie and music stars do it too so…. I promise I will not let it get out of control. I will only do it sometimes, like for fun or on special occasions.

"No, and that's final yo. I've watched too many girls throw their life away over this shit." I rolled my eyes. Rod got up from the couch to go into our bedroom. I followed him. "What do you have planned today?"

I shrugged my shoulders, "Cleaning up is about it, why? What do you want to do today?"

"I told my mom you'll stop by before her and my dad leave for Hawaii."

"Wait, what? You're not going with me?" I sat on our bed.

"I might stop by, but I got…"

"A run to make," I said mockingly, cutting him off.

"Don't fucking do that yo, I hate that shit."

"You always have a run to make. When was the last time you spent time with your parents?"

"My parents understand there is money to be make out here."

"It's always about money with you."

"Why are you making this into a thing?"

"Because you have your parents Rod, I don't. I wish for another day, hell another minute with them. You are taking your parents for granted," I began to get emotional, I didn't intend to it just happened. But it was the truth.

"Baby, I'm sorry. I've never looked at it like that."

"At the end of the day memories will be the only thing we will have to cling on to, that is why it's important to make memories now because memories can't be replaced."

"I get it yo, sometimes I forget how much you've endured," Rod kissed my forehead. "How about this, by the time you get dressed I'll be back from this drop and then we can go see my parents off, is that cool?" I nodded in agreement. I don't want him taking his parents for granted. He must spend time with them while he still can. We stayed at his parents' house for a couple of hours before it was time for them to catch their flight. Mr. Quentin was cracking jokes about how they weren't coming back from their paradise. Mrs. Robin looked so worried and excited at the same time. Before leaving they made sure to lay down the law. Although their children are all grown, there still is a glimmer of mistrust. They never said when they would be returning, but they stressed the fact to not have a house full of people. They don't have to worry about that on me and Rod's part because we have our own apartment and we do what we please over there. Hugs and kisses were given to each of us then they left. I texted Emory. She didn't come to the house this evening and since all the other significant others were there, I'm worried about her. Rod and I stayed in his old room for a little while. His room is still intact from the first day I walked into it. I sat in the chaise. I ran my hand over the tears that I'd made from our first fight. Rod and I have come a long way. We still argue, but we made a promise to never put hands on one another again. He paced around the room, I bet he misses being here. It's nothing like your childhood home, so many memories. I still miss our home back in Georgia.

"Are you ready to go home?" I asked Rod.

"I have to make some more stops first," he joined me on the chaise.

I rested my head on his chest, "I want to do something."

"Like what?"

"I don't know, let's go to the movies or something. I just want to spend time with you, without you having to leave to make a run. The only time we spend together is when we're having sex."

"We spend plenty of time together. Stop acting like me making runs is new, I've been doing this shit since we've been together. We can go to the movies, but not tonight."

I sighed, "Well take me home."

"Chill with the attitude, yo," he raised his voice.

"Can you please take me home?" I said more calmly.

"Iight," he dropped me off at our apartment. He didn't even come inside, he just sped off once I was out the car. I guess I'm stuck entertaining myself tonight, as usual. I cleaned the house top to bottom. I prepped tomorrow's dinner. I marinated chicken thighs in coconut pineapple sauce. I made sure I had all the ingredients for baked macaroni and cheese, and I'll cook the rice tomorrow.

A text message came through to my phone. 'Coffee?' I figured the message was from the guy, Xavier from the party. I could use something a lot stronger than coffee right now, but I confirmed that I would meet him at the coffee shop by the mall. I felt horrible from the encounter I just had with Rod, but I put on my best smile when I walked into the shop. Xavier smiled at me and motioned for me to join him. He was nibbling on a pastry but stood as I got closer. He looked even more handsome than last night. He held the chair out for me to sit, "I was beginning to think you had stood me up," he said after taking his seat.

I smiled, "I wouldn't do that," I made him wait on purpose. I didn't want to seem desperate to see him.

"Did you have to sneak away?" I searched his face looking for a clue to how he knows something about me that I didn't tell him. He smiled before adding, "I've done my research."

"Why research when you can get facts directly from the source?"

"That's true, but I still had to find out what I was getting myself into."

Normally, shit like this would piss me off, but I maintained my composure. "Entertain me, what did you find out about little ole me?" The barista called his name. He returned with two cups of coffee. I can't believe he ordered for me. He sat the cup in front of me. He waited until I grabbed the cup and we sipped our drinks at the same time. I smirked once the flavor of the hot coffee hit my tongue.

"For starters, I know your favorite coffee is white chocolate mocha," not too many people know that about me. I rarely drink coffee, but when I do it has to be white chocolate mocha. My mind raced as I wondered who the hell this man has been talking to.

"Okay, I'm officially freaked out," could I possibly be sitting across from my stalker? "Who have you been talking to?" I took another sip anticipating his answer.

"Your sister, I know her through Ray. I'm Ray's best friend. After the party I told her I was interested in you."

"If you're cool with Ray then you should know…"

"You're Rod's girlfriend. Yes, Shae informed me, but that doesn't make me less interested. Everybody's been talking about you and Rod, but last night was my first time seeing you. Why isn't he showing you off?"

I became uneasy, "Why do I have to be seen?"

"Mainly because that's Rod's M.O."

"I don't need nor want the entire New Bern knowing our business." Which is half a lie, I do want him to flaunt me around sometimes. Only to let these bitches know that I do exist and I'm his one and only. Then again, that is his responsible to let them know that. I'm in a losing battle if he doesn't take that initiative.

"I hear you," Xavier replied. He finished his coffee and his pastry. I haven't been here ten minutes and his questioning were irritating me. If I wanted to talk about me and Rod, I'll go talk to Rod. I finished my own coffee, I was over this coffee date. "Can we still talk?"

"If it's anything about Rod, no, but if you'll like to talk to me about me then, yes."

A smile graced his handsome face. "I really want to get to know you."

"Well?" I questioned.

"Would you like another cup of coffee?"

"No, I've had enough."

"I'll tell you about me," he cleared his throat. "I'm a painter,"

"That bartends at parties," I added.

"Sometimes. Um...my father is a preacher at a small church. We have conflicting outlooks on my future. I'm single. What else?"

"Baby mamas?" I blurted.

"None."

"Back to your father, does he not approve of you wanting to be a painter?"

"Naw, I'm the oldest and he believes I should follow in his footsteps. My passion is painting, I love what I create."

"How many siblings do you have?"

"It's just me and my brother, Kace."

"What about your mom?"

He sighed heavily, "She left us when I was five, I don't really remember her anymore."

"What are you going to do about your father?"

He shrugged, "I have faith that it'll get better and work itself out. I've heard about your parents, I'm sorry."

"It's okay, thank you. So, what do you paint?"

"Anything, I'm really into oil painting, but I've worked with pastels and watercolor as well. I just like to get my hands dirty. I paint still objects, sunsets, and people."

"People? Hm."

He smiled, "Are you going to let me paint you?"

I laughed, "I bet you say that to all the girls, huh?" A message came in from Emory saying she will call me.

"Do you have to go?"

"I don't *have* to go, but I do need to get going. It's getting late."

"When are you free?"

"Everyday. You can text me anytime," I gathered my things to leave.

"Your man won't have a problem with that?"

"We'll see," I gave him a friendly embrace before leaving the coffee shop. Xavier seems really cool, but what concerns me is his connection to the Hill family. I'm not trying to sneak around with him like that, I think we can be friends. Maybe, I'm trying to fill the void of that male friendship like I had with Aaron. I'll never leave Rod. I called Emory when I got into the car, she didn't sound like herself, I stared at the phone for a second making sure I dialed the correct number. "Em?" I asked. I plugged my phone into the speakers as I drove off. I could hear her crying and that hurt me. "What's wrong?"

"He's still fucking that bitch, Siah," she said in between the sobs. I could feel her pain through the phone. "He was mad that I went to that party. I just left his house, he's drunk as hell so he's rambling and shit. He slipped and said it."

"Are you sure, maybe he's just saying that shit to make you mad," I tried to make it better for her.

"No, he knows how I am. That shit slipped out his fucking mouth, I don't even think he knows he said it. He's so fucked up off pills and shit. I'm done. I'm done fighting bitches over him for him to only go back to sticking in dick in them."

I didn't know what to say, what advise could I give anyway? It's like we are always back in this cycle. If it's not her, it's me. "Let's just get away," I suggested.

"Where? Because at this point, I would like to be anywhere but here. I can't take this anymore. I thought about calling my aunt in Charlotte, but I don't feel like dealing with her lurking ass husband."

"Pack a bag for a couple of days, I'll pick you up in a few hours." Emory agreed, and honestly, I don't know where we should go. As her friend, it's my job to allow her to escape every once and awhile. I've decided once I got home to not tell Rod about Emory going out of town with me. I'm sure he would tell Chris and I have a feeling that she doesn't want him to know where she is going. Hell, I don't know where we're going. Rod was in the shower when I got home, I joined him. I made love to him. The passion this man possesses is intoxicating.

"What did I do to deserve that?" He asked as we were drying off.

I kissed him, "I just love you."

"What do you want, Si? Keep it straight."

Damn, he sees right through me. "I'm going out of town for a couple of days."

"Hmm...where?" I followed him to the bedroom.

"I'll let you know when I get there."

"The fuck does that mean, yo? Naw, you can't go."

"I wasn't asking. I'm leaving tonight and I will call you to let you know where I end up." I packed my clothes for the trip. He stood in front of me anticipating an argument. I embraced him in the most loving way.

He wrapped his arms around me, "You're not leaving me, are you? I'm sorry about earlier," he whispered into my ear.

"No, it's just a quick trip. I'll be back before you know it."

"Iight, call me yo," I kissed my man.

I picked Emory up from her parent's house. On the way over I decided we should just go to Effingham for many reasons. I don't know people anywhere else, plus I want to see Aaron and I want to pick up some essentials that I can't get in North Carolina. I texted Aaron about coming and he said he'd prepare a room for me. I didn't tell Emory where we were going, I just drove the entire way. The interstate at night isn't as busy with cars. I used to hate driving at night, but now I find it peaceful. Emory slept the entire way, she is exhausted from all the crying. We have got to stop letting these niggas have this much control over our emotions. Love or not, all we ask for is for them to make us happy. Why should we have to shed so many fucking tears over the shit they put us through? I'm tired of crying and I'm tired of seeing Emory cry. I nudged her once I pulled in front of Aaron's apartment building.

"Where are we?" She asked yawning and stretching.

"Aaron's house, remember I told you about him?" Olivia opened the door when we knocked. For her to be up at this hour she had to be the one respond to the text I sent Aaron. She was probably up going through his phone like always.

"Hey Aaron, I'm Emory," she extended her hand to Olivia.

I fought back a snicker, "Em, this is actually Aaron's girlfriend, Olivia."

"Fiancé," she corrected me while shaking Emory's hand.

I disregarded her comment because had it been any truth behind it, Aaron would have definitely called me, "Where's Aaron?"

"He's asleep, but I've made arrangements. I'm sorry, I thought you were coming alone. So, one can sleep on the couch and the other can take the spare room."

"No, we prefer to sleep together," Emory said. I smiled because her silly ass made it sound like we actually sleep together.

"Oh. Okay," Olivia showed us to the room. "Let me know if you need anything. The bathroom is down the hall on the left."

"Thank you," I did appreciate Olivia for her hospitality. She closed the door behind her.

"What's her deal?" I shrugged. I laid down because I'm tired as fuck.

Refreshed and ready to enjoy this trip. I noticed Emory made herself useful by unpacking the car. While she was M.I.A, I decided to call Rod. "Hey Baby," he answered. "Where are you?"

"I came to Georgia. I'll be here for a couple of days."

"That's fine Baby be safe," he yawned. We talked for a couple more minutes. He better miss me while I'm gone. I went out the room to search for Emory. I found her eating breakfast with Olivia.

"Good Morning, where is Aaron?"

"In the bedroom," she said with a mouth full.

I barged into his room, "Well damn, hello best friend." I stood with my arms folded.

"Hey, I didn't know you were coming."

"But you knew I was here, and it's almost noon."

"So, I'm supposed to just coming running. Face it, it's been months since we've last held a conversation. You're only here now because you need something from me, what about when I need you?"

"What?! I've always been here, you're the one who stopped calling me." I yelled at him. He's trying my patience. Aaron and I fuss a lot. It comes from growing up together and being around each other so much. We know how to push each other's buttons. I give him a hard time because we made promises before I left Georgia. Nothing is supposed to get in the way of our friendship.

He slammed the door shut. "Bullshit, I call every Thursday as promised. Your phone goes straight to voicemail."

"No, your number hasn't been on my call log since the last time I was here to get Kennon."

"Your *man* must have blocked my number," Aaron sat on his bed like he had it all figured out.

"Why would he do that?" *IF* Rod did such a thing, we were going to have a problem when I get back home.

He shrugged his shoulders, "I don't know, but he must feel some type of way about me being your friend."

"Shut up, like your *fiancé* doesn't have a problem with us being friends."

"She doesn't," he lied. Olivia has always tried to swindle her way into Aaron's life. Back in high school she was only a one-night stand that turned psycho when he stopped returning her phone calls. He treated her badly, and I did feel bad. But back in the day Aaron was all about who he can fuck, that's it. And sad to say she was only a number to him. Of course, she felt some type of way because he and I were so close, she swore up and down I had something to do with him ignoring her.

"Yeah, whatever. This engagement true?" He nodded. "Congratulations."

"Thanks, so how long are you here for?"

"Until you get tired of me," we laughed. I stood against the room door. I can't believe he asked that chick to marry him. Never in my life did I imagine marriage being in Aaron's vocabulary. We stared at each other for a good minute. We have grown so much in so little time. Aaron came to me, he looked deeply into my eyes as he unbuckled the button on my jeans. "Aaron, are you crazy?" He shushed me. He kissed me and I kissed him back. We were hungry for each other. He locked the door then carried me to his bed. He removed my jeans and underwear, exposing my shaven pussy. As he spread my legs a smile crept across his face. He licked his lips then proceeded to feast on my honey jar I wanted to push him away, but my body was responding to his tongue and touches. I moaned as he licked me in ways I've never been licked before. I panicked thinking at any moment his fiancé would barge through the door. "Aaron, Olivia is right down the hall," I struggled to say, but his head never left from between my legs. I came, he knelt between my legs stroking his massive dick. He slid inside of me quickly. I moaned his name. He held my legs up to the ceiling as his dick slid in and out of me. The bed was creaking loudly, but he didn't seem to care about the noise. We changed positions, he sat up as I rode him my titties bouncing in his face. He held onto my waist as I slid up and down his dick. He smiled as we both came. We quickly got dressed just in case Olivia came to the door.

"You don't know how long I've wanted to do that," Aaron said.

"I can't believe we just did that."

"Why not? You know how I feel about you." He lifted my chin to kiss me. In some way I've always been attracted to Aaron. We've just been friends for so long that I pushed the attraction aside. I've always told myself we are friends, and nothing will ever happen between us, but here I am. I just fucked my best friend, and I enjoyed it.

"You're getting married."

"You don't even care for her."

"Not the point, plus we're best friends," I whined.

"Siah, I literally just took my dick out of you and now you're regretting it." I hung my head, "Wow! I have to go to work. We can talk later."

"I don't regret it. I just don't want that," I pointed to the bed like we were still over there smashing. "To fuck up our friendship."

"And it won't. We can be mature about this." He kissed me again passionately letting his tongue slide against mine. He began to suckle on my neck.

A knock at the door, "Are y'all coming to eat breakfast or just fuss all day?" Olivia said through the door.

"We're almost done," Aaron answered her. I heard her footsteps retreat to the kitchen.

"Are we almost done?" I seduced him by undoing his zipper. I played with his huge dick until it was rock hard. He moaned against my ear. I jerked him off until he came into my hand. We shared another passionate kiss. Aaron's dick was actually the first one I've ever seen. Touching it and feeling it inside me for the first time is amazing.

"I'll see you around 8 o'clock when I get off," I washed my hands in their bathroom sink.

"Not going to eat breakfast?"

"I already ate," I followed him out the room. He kissed Olivia goodbye and I joined Emory at the table.

"Wait, Aaron," what are we doing for dinner tonight?" Olivia asked.

"Siah, do you still make those bomb ass hot wings?"

"Yes, she does," Emory answered for me. I made them one Saturday she and Chris came over. Needless to say, that night there wasn't any leftovers. Emory and Chris demolished the wings and took to go plates.

"Let's have that," Aaron handed me his credit card to grab the ingredients I need. I noticed Olivia side eyeing me. When he left out the door, reality set in. I made it through breakfast, but the entire time I was thinking about what I've just done with my best friend. I'm sitting across from this girl knowing that her man just cheated on her with me. And I've cheated on Rod. The sex was good though, and I've known Aaron for forever. It won't be weird. This is something that I will most definitely keep to myself. What will I tell Rod anyway? In the beginning of our relationship I assured him that Aaron and I were only friends, and up until an hour ago we were. What changed? If Aaron was into me before, why didn't he say anything before? I became angry with Aaron. Just infuriated with him in my mind.

"Siah?" Olivia snapped me back to reality. I couldn't bear to look at her. I almost hate myself for what I did to her. I'm no better than the bitches that be in Rod's face.

"I'm sorry, yes?" I drank the remainder of my coffee.

"Here is a key to the apartment. Emory mentioned you guys were going to go shopping. I have to get to work so now you can let yourselves in. I'll be returning around ten-thirty and Aaron should be back at seven or eight. I can't wait to taste these hot wings!" She rushed out leaving the key on the countertop. I'm glad she's gone.

Emory and I went to Springfield just to sight see. So much has changed in the little time I've been gone. We went back to Rincon to shop for shoes and clothes. I also got my favorite sodas and bottled water that New Bern or surrounding areas fail to have. We ate lunch at my favorite spot. I love being here. I'd powered my phone completely off, so I didn't have to talk to Rod. I have so much going on in my head that I need time to clear it before I can talk to him. Back at Aaron's apartment, Emory helped me cook the hot wings before Olivia and Aaron came home. We chose to have sweet potato fries as the side dish. Emory's been on this healthy kick lately and monitors everything I eat. Emory and I sat at opposite ends of the couch, sharing a blanket we found in the room as we watched a movie. Once they got home, we shared the meal at their dinner table. We ended up playing UNO first then Monopoly. After the games ended, Emory retreated to the room, she said she had to check in with her parents. I figured she was probably going to call Chris. But to each its own. It's her life. I powered my phone on then texted Rod to see what he was up to. Alone in the dark living room, my thoughts were loud in my head. What have I gotten myself into? When I get home, I'm going to tell Rod everything that way no secrets are between us.

Aaron joined me on the couch, "Why are you sitting in the dark?" He asked, but I shrugged my shoulders. "Let's go for a walk." We walked up and down the small street talking about life. We discussed Olivia and Rod as we gave each other advice. Our conversations were strictly friendly and I'm glad our rendezvous didn't change anything. Although, my attraction for him is stronger than ever before. We love and want the best for each other no matter what. Emory was sound asleep when I stepped into the room. I put her phone and mine on the charger. I don't know about her, but I am ready to get back home. She cannot run from her problems for too long, it's time to face the music. I lay beside her. I'll tell her the news about going home in the morning.

In the morning, Aaron took me to breakfast. Emory was still asleep, so I didn't wake her to invite her. I made up my mind that we would spend one more day in Georgia. Rod hadn't texted me back from last night and it has me worried. I sent another text to him. Aaron and I pretty much hung out the entire morning. We went by his parents' house, and they were so excited to see me, and I was ecstatic to see them. His mom kept hugging me, and at one point we were holding hands. His mom, just like my mom would have, pried all into my personal business, but growing up with this lady I happily told her what I wanted her to know. I got deep with her because she always loved our girl talks. She advised me to be careful with dealing with any man that deals drug. She said drug money is so attractive to females and some men cannot resist the attention they get because of it. I took in every word she said to me. She also told me to protect my heart at all costs and I intend to do just that.

"I like how you left me," Emory sarcastically said to me. I handed her the Chinese food I got for her.

"Sorry, I kinda wanted a day with Aaron before we leave."

"You've been hanging with Aaron the entire time we've been here," she pouted. "I thought this getaway was for me."

"Aww, you're jealous. Emory, you wanted to get away and you have. You're both my best friend, but I don't get to see him as often as I used to."

"Well we should have all spent time together. I felt excluded."

"I'm sorry, that was not my intention. We are leaving in the morning, then you'll have me all to yourself."

"Until Rod calls," she rolled her eyes playfully. Emory and I spent the remainder of the day watching movies and talking about our love life. She told me once again that she has decided to forgive Chris and give him another chance. I said the same words to her that Aaron's mom said to me: protect your heart.

CHAPTER 14

The second we drove across the North Carolina state line our phones dinged. Since Emory was driving, I looked at both our phones. Both displayed a text from the same number. A number I couldn't help but remember: Yazzy's.

"Who is it from?" Emory tried to look over to see. I moved the phones from her eyes sight. I have a feeling about these text messages, and it isn't good.

"Focus on the road, it's from Yazzy. We only have a few more hours of driving so we can ignore it for now," I turned the music up. We ended up going to my siblings' house. Since Rod doesn't deem it important to text or call me back, I don't deem it important to let him know I'm back in town.

I turned on the candle wax warmer in my old room to freshen the musky air. We also smoked a blunt she had rolled. We sat on the bed with our phones in hand then counted to three to open the message from Yazzy. It was a video. Once it played, I knew exactly why she'd sent it to me. The video was so low quality, but I made out what she wanted me to see. It was her and Rod, she was kissing all over the tattoo he'd gotten of my name a month ago. Of all the tattoos on his body she decided to kiss on the one with my fucking name. Then I saw her hand rubbing his penis through his pants. I could hear him saying, 'Stop, yo' if you don't plan on doing shit,' he had no idea she was recording him.

Emory let out a yelp, I had nearly forgot she was in the room. "Si, look at this shit," There was Yazzy again on her screen. Only this time she was giving Chris head. Obviously, a video they both participated in recording. As the video went on Chris pleased Yazzy orally as well. The comment under Emory's video read, 'He'll NEVER stop fucking with me.' I checked the comment beneath mine, and it read, 'Just know I can have him whenever I want.' I handed the phone back to Emory, "The nerve of this bitch, she acts like I won't go beat her ass. She lucky this shit is mad old."

"What do you mean?"

"About a year ago, Chris was smoking out of glass pipe and it dropped on his inner thigh. The mark never went away, and in this pixelated ass video it's not there. I'm still pissed at how he's been fucking with her for this long."

I showed her the video Yazzy sent to me, "This video is recent. Rod just added my name to his tattoos."

"Damn, Bitch, he got your name tatted on him? What's your secret?" She joked, but I wasn't in a joking mood.

I turned my phone over, "I'm not feeding into her shit, that bitch don't even deserve a response." I'll deal with Rod's ass later, I thought to myself.

After an hour and four blunts later, I sent a text. Once I got the response I wanted I left Emory at the house. Xavier met me outside his apartment complex. "What's up?" He opened the car door. "How was your trip?"

"Great," he texted me when I was in Georgia. We've had several long texting conversations. I talked to him more than I talked to Rod on the trip.

He led the way up to the apartment, "My brother, Kace is here too by the way."

"And?"

"I'm just letting you know." Their apartment smelt of weed, but it was simply decorated with Jamaica's flag colors. A portrait of Bob Marley hung on the walls above the black leather sofas. A keyboard piano was tucked in the corner of the room. Kace was sitting on the sofa watching football on the big screen tv. Xavier introduced us. "Do you want anything to drink?"

"Oh, yes Mr. Bartender," Kace laughed at my comment, "Do you have rum?"

He checked in the kitchen for the liquor, "Naw, we got vodka though. Would you like it with cranberry juice?"

"No, I'll take it straight."

"Damn, what kind of day have you had?" Kace spoke, but his eyes were glued to the game.

"A very long one," I said answering his question. I grabbed the drink from Xavier.

"Let's go to my room," he said to me. We walked down the short hallway. In his room was artwork everywhere. My eyes went directly to the canvasses leaning against the wall. I took a big gulp of my drink before setting it on the table beside his bed. Paintings of numerous of girls in provocative positions. Seeing these painting turned me on. Girls legs were spread wide, and he captured the essence of their vaginas. He painted boobs so realistic. I could be jumping the gun, but it almost seems like every nigga in New Bern is a hoe. It could be just work to him. He has some scenery paintings as well. No lie he has talent and I just might let him paint me.

"How many of these girls in these paintings have you had sex with?" I asked boldly with my liquor courage.

"None. They pay me for those paintings some for their husband, boyfriends, or girlfriends."

"How much do you charge?"

"It depends."

"On if they are fully clothed or not?"

"Yeah," I laughed as I finished my drink. I laid on his bed. "I'm waiting on you to tell me which one you want to do."

"I think I would rather do fully clothed unless it's going to be a present for my man then I would consider a fully nude painting of me."

"Well either way I can make it happen."

"I will keep that in mind," I sat on his bed. I wonder what those girls that posed for the painting were thinking. Married, involved or not, they have some strong will power to be sitting in front of his fine ass without clothes and not do anything with him.

"So, you know my talent, what is yours?"

I shrugged, "I don't know anymore. I wanted to do so many different things in my life, but life happened, and it caused me to change how I view things. I will figure it out one day."

"My advice is to always do something you enjoy, no need in wasting your time." I agree with this statement.

"What is your brother's talent."

Xavier hesitated for a moment, "he sells, that's why he and my dad don't see eye to eye."

"Your dad's not talking to you or your brother?"

"Well me and my dad talk we just have different opinions on what I should do with my life, but it doesn't affect our relationship too much. I still try to have a conversation with him every now and again because he's the only parent that I have contact with.

"How did your brother get into selling drugs? It seems like a common theme in New Bern."

"I told you before we're real close with the Hill family *your* man recruited him. I don't sell that shit, but I do smoke it. Liquor is my choice." He smiled, "What is one thing people confuse you and your sister with that is totally off base"

"Probably the sex thing. Before she got with Raymond she was out there, and all the guys thought I was the same. Before I moved here, I'd never had sex."

"Rod's your first?" I nodded.

"Damn," I could see his demeanor change a little. Almost like he was contemplating his next move.

"I don't like talking about Rod with you."

"Why not? It helps me to find out what my chances are."

"Who says you have a chance?"

"Well you are at my house in my bed, so I'd say I got a chance."

"I don't know maybe we will see."

"I want to find out what my chances are right now," Xavier kissed me, and I accepted him fully in an instant my pants were off with Xavier's hand in my honey jar. I softly moaned. I shouldn't have let this go as far as it has, but I'm loving the feeling of his fingers inside me. I need to feel complete. He tasted my juices on his fingertips then he laid all the way down pulling me on top of him until my pussy was over his face. Xavier gobbled me up. I rode his face and you would've thought I was suffocating him. My moans were so loud I didn't care that his brother was in the next room. His tongue was taking me places giving me orgasm after orgasm. We switched positions, he laid me down on my back, he was taking special care of my breasts, kissing my neck and fingering me he leaned over to his pants on the floor to grab a condom out of his wallet. He rolled it on his fully erect penis before he slid inside of me. We had excellent sex I mean he had me in positions I've never tried before. "I'm sorry, I couldn't help myself." Xavier said once we were finished, I covered my naked body with his covers. I've now had sex with three guys, and it seems like it gets better each time. At this point, I don't care about Rod and how he feels because he doesn't care about me and how I feel. Xavier said, "What time do you have to leave?"

I sat up, "I have to get back to Emory that's all. Rod doesn't even know I'm back in town."

"How about you just tell Emory to come over here. I want more time with you."

I didn't like that idea, but I do want to spend more time with him. I'm just not sure how Emory will be able to keep this secret from Chris. All hell will break loose if Rod found out I'm hanging with Xavier. He'll try to kill Xavier if he finds out about the sex we just had. But I sent the text to her anyway along with the address. Xavier and I went into the living room to await her arrival.

"You ditched me for Xavier?" Emory said as she walked into the apartment. She sat on the couch with Kace. "What's going on? Do ya'll have some bud?"

"What kind of question is that?" Kace asked her, he lit the blunt that was sitting on the coffee table. We passed it around the room, we got hella high off that one blunt.

Xavier leaned over like he was about to whisper something to me, but he started to kiss my neck. I folded into him, my back pressed against the arm of the couch. I held onto the cusp of his face as he suckled on my neck. I moaned lightly. "Let's go back to my room," he whispered to me. When I got up, I noticed Kace and Emory were no longer on the other couch.

"Where is Em?" I asked Xavier.

"In Kace's room, she'll be fine. They know each other." Xavier and I completed round two, three and four. My pussy was his tonight and she was loving the way he filled her. He made the handsomest faces when he comes. "Am I going to see you after tonight?"

"Of course, you're going to see a lot of me." I smiled at him. I looked at my phone to check the time, 2:49 a.m. I noticed a text from Rod. '*I can't wait until you get home.*' It read, and I immediately sent him the video that Yazzy sent to me. I put the phone on vibrate then laid against Xavier's chest. I did not want to involve him in this drama. Yes, I'm still with Rod, but not for long. I'm willing to leave him to be with Xavier. It's only a matter of time before I let him know.

Emory and I left Xavier and Kace's apartment before the sun came up. Talk about the ultimate walk of shame. We didn't say anything on the way to my sibling's house, but when we got into the room, we burst out laughing. We shared a good laugh for five minutes straight. Probably shocked that we just cheated on our boyfriends. "Siah, we have to keep that shit to ourselves."

"You're telling me? Bitch, when did you move from the couch last night?"

"After we smoked that blunt, you know how I get." She sat on the floor, "Plus, Kace and I have always had this physical attraction. I've been so scared to fuck with him, but Baby when I tell you. That boy's dick is so fucking good. Like, me and his dick are best friends now," we laughed again. "How was Xavier?"

I blushed, "It was good, too good."

"We have to be careful though, they are entirely too close to Rod, Chris and Raymond. I got your back and I know you have mine."

"Yes, of course. I do want to end this relationship with Rod," I spoke truthfully.

"And I want to be single for a while. These last days with you have been the best days I've had in years. I know I can live without Chris and the way he cheats on me. I have to value myself more, thank you for being my inspiration." She stood to hug me. I don't know where this is coming from, but I'm glad we both see the light at the end of the Hill boy's tunnel.

Rod has been calling my phone all morning trying to reach me. I think I'm ready to talk to him now. Since Emory had to check in with her parents, I took that time to go to the apartment Rod and I share. He was sitting in the living room when I walked into the door, "Si, I can explain that video," he stood to face me.

"Please do," I waited for him to try to lie his way out of this situation.

"I didn't fuck her," he said.

"That's you explaining the video?" I walked past him to the sit on the couch. "You let her touch all on your dick. You might as well had fucked the bitch."

"I was drunk."

I smacked my teeth, "Okay, well I don't want to be with you Rod. She has too much control and access to you."

"I didn't fuck her," he stared out the window. He couldn't look me in the eyes because he's probably lying.

"You didn't fuck her when? That night? Because you have fucked that bitch," I could feel myself start to lose my cool.

"Si, I haven't touched that girl since we've been together. I was drunk as fuck that night. She wouldn't have done that shit if I were sober."

"It's whatever. I'm done because it's disrespectful drunk or not."

He glared at me, "You're done with me?"

"Yep," I folded my arms.

"So, saying you love me and will never leave me, was just a lie, right?" He began to tear up, "You don't care about what I have to say. You're always believing these outside bitches." He covered his eyes with his hands. I felt bad. I did promise I would never leave him, but I am breaking that promise. All I require of him is for him to do right by me, no bitches, no cheating. Just love me the way I deserve to be loved. I wouldn't have run to Aaron or Xavier if he'd been treating me right. I watched him cry softly.

"Rod, I did promise those things, and I meant them. I can only take so much and right now I'm at my breaking point. I love you, but I cannot continue like this." It took everything in me not to hug him tight, take him into our room to make love to him.

"Please, don't leave me."

"It's time to have a chat with this bitch,"

"What?" He tried to protest.

"No, if you want to be with me this has to happen. Let's go," I grabbed his car keys and rushed out the door. I knocked on her apartment door, it was so tempting to slap the shit out of her when she answered, but I refrained. "What's up Yazzy?" I asked. She looked like she was going to piss her pants.

She looked at Rod, then me, "Why are you here?"

"The video you sent, you wanted a reaction. Here I am, speak up, say what you have to say."

"I was just letting you know how your man acts over here."

"How I act?" Rod came onto the stoop, "How is that Yaz?"

She snickered, "Come on, let's not get amnesia because Siah is here." She turned back to me, "bitches be all over him and he allows it, and that wasn't me in the video."

Confused because I assumed it was her, "Who was it?"

She looked at him and he glared at her, "Siah, despite us not being on speaking terms, I still care for you."

I held my hand up, fuck what she was talking about, I looked at him, "Who was in that video?"

"Teana," he and I said in unison.

I chuckled, I turned to Yazzy, "Next time, don't hit my line with no bullshit. I don't give a fuck what you know because next time…. next time I won't be so nice," I walked away with poise. Rod followed trying to plead his case. Right then I should've blurted out that I fucked Aaron and Xavier. Right then I should have made him hurt the way I've been hurting. I walked back to the avenue. I needed to collect my thoughts. I told Rod that if he followed me, I was going to call the cops. I got a text from Xavier requesting to see me. I told him later. I don't want to be around any nigga right now. A blunt is much needed, but Emory's at her house and I don't want to be alone.

Heartbreak, deceit, and unfaithfulness, my parents did not prepare me for this. I don't know how to handle it all. Loving someone who cheats, being forced to cheat myself. Payback is a powerful bitch, but I have yet to scratch the surface.

I pulled up to Emory's house in Fort Tot, which is literally streets over from the avenue. Emory has never invited me over house because she is never there, she met me outside once I pulled up in the driveway.

"Hey girl, my parents want to meet you," she said as if it was a bad thing. I followed her into the house, "Mom, Dad, this is my best friend La'Siah."

"Nice to finally meet you," her dad said we shook hands. "Emory is very secretive about her friends nowadays. She tells us that you're with Tyrrod."

I chuckled, "Yes, you can say that."

"We've been asking her for months to introduce us because we want to know who she's hanging with. You can never be too careful in this town. But at one point we thought she was seeing another boy besides Chris."

"Okay, that's enough Dad," little Emory was getting embarrassed.

"Mom, have you seen my charger?" A guy said as he approached the kitchen. "Oh, shit Em, I didn't know you were here."

"*I* actually live here," she rolled her eyes at him. "Siah, this is my annoying big brother…"

"Zo," I said before she could say anything. This is the same nigga I delivered to for Rod. What a small ass world.

Emory looked between us then it clicked in her mind, "Yes he goes by Zo, but his real name is Khalil. Zo is his street name."

"Noted," I said. I smiled at Khalil, also known as Zo. It did seem weird that he was not in a gangster setting as I have seen him before.

"Dad, I'm staying at Siah's house tonight if that's cool." I don't mind Emory staying nights with me, but she could consult me first.

I have a lot of issues that I need to deal with plus I have plans to go see Xavier.

"Emory you haven't been home in a week," her mom said to her.

"I'm not a child anymore," she said shrugging it off.

"Why ask if you can stay? That what children do," Khalil said to his sister.

"Khalil, shut up," she snapped at him. I snickered Emory drug me away quickly.

"Nice to meet you all," I called out. We settled in her beautiful decorated room. King sized swing bed rested against the turquoise painted wall, everything was neatly in place. I flopped on her bed just like she does mine. "What's the deal with you not wanting to be home?"

"I don't know, I just feel like I am grown, and I need to be out of my own they hardly let me do anything besides go to Chris' house. That's why I didn't tell them about you because they would make every excuse for you to come over here so we can be here all the time. They are very protective. When Chris and I first started dating, they had to have a sit down with Mr. Q and Mrs. Robin. To talk about their little girl." She rolled her eyes, "They are embarrassing sometimes."

"So, your brother is Zo, why didn't you tell me before? I asked changing the subject. Even after I told her about the run I made for Rod she didn't disclose that information with me. I'm glad I didn't say anything bad about him.

"I thought maybe Rod would have told you that my brother is his plug. Plus, Zo isn't always around. He is in and out of jail because he gets caught having ounces on him. This is the longest he's been out, maybe he got smarter." She shrugged, "He's just another reason my parents try to put a tight leash on me."

After a moment of silence, I told Emory about what just transpired between me Yazzy and Rod. She was floored and wished that I have taken her with me and so that way she could beat the shit out of Yazzy, but that wouldn't do any good. I needed to get my things out of our apartment, and I needed it out as soon as possible. I want to close that door on Rod's chapter as soon as possible.

Emory and I rode around New Bern smoking. She let Khalil ride with us only because he had the weed. After about the third blunt and the fifth ride through The Bricks I got the courage to go to the apartment because sometimes you need to some forgive, forget, then let go. Emory drove us back to her house, but before I could go to Rod, I made a quick pit stop. I was presented with a proposition and I'm curious to see where it may lead. The way Khalil was looking at me when I entered the hotel room was everything, but I don't know if I'm ready to take on another dope boy. Plus, he is Emory's brother and she gets jealous if she has to share me with anyone. One night of passion is what I keep telling myself. It's like a test drive. He kept murmuring under his breath how he wanted to taste me. Why not? With his head in between my legs, I felt like I was wasting my time. He's not the best at eating pussy, but at this moment in time I needed him. After that horrible encounter, my mind went to racing again about Rod. Honestly, I do forgive him for trying to play me because now, I've gotten my revenge. I was dead wrong thinking I could change him into the man I needed him to be, but that shit is on me. It'll take me awhile to forget it all because I do love him so much, but you're not supposed to hurt the ones you love. The huge part, letting go. Rod will always have a place in my heart because he is my first love, and not to mention my first heartbreak. This is a hard pill to swallow. Losing my parents taught me to love like it was my last day on earth and I gave that man all I have. I've run dry and empty, I don't have anything else to give.

"Talk to me baby," he said to me when I entered the cold, lonely apartment. The way he calls me baby made me weak. I tried to keep the reason why I'm moving in my mind.

"What can you explain that I don't already know?" I asked him. I grabbed my suitcase from the closet I had to get my clothes, everything else can wait until I find boxes.

He lit a blunt, "You want to hit it?" he asked.

"You think you can tempt me with weed?" He just disregards my feelings. Is it too much to ask for him to try to make it better? Stop making excuses for things and figure out how we can fix us.

Just explain shit to me so I'm not in the dark. All I have to cling on is what my mind has created about his infidelities.

He shrugged his shoulders, "it got you talking." He took a long drag of the blunt filled with weed.

"Say what you have to say Rod," I stopped packing to give him my attention.

"I know I fucked up, but you have to believe me when I say I didn't fuck her. I can't explain shit right now, but I promise I've never cheated on you."

"Okay, I believe you."

He looked shocked, "Do you really Yo? Or are you just saying that shit?"

"Yeah," I said, "I believe you want me to think that. Right now, I don't care because you present yourself as a single man. If we're supposed to be together, you have to act accordingly. And this isn't the first incident that we've had with this bitch Teana. You claim she's an ex, but the way you keep her hanging around, I think differently."

"I act single?" He fired back, "What about you, huh?"

"Everybody in New Bern knows I'm with you, so who do I ask single around?" I put my hands on my hips.

"My nigga at the coffee spot says he seen you and Xavier together, what was that shit about?"

"I had coffee with a friend," I said plainly. He's reaching. He knows he doesn't have shit on me because I made sure of it. Unlike him, I make sure to cover my steps.

"Friend?" He smirked, he put the blunt out. "How long have you known that nigga?

"Not long," I stirred the pot by giving him this short answer. Funny how he wants answers, but I can't get any answers from him.

"So how the fuck is he your friend?" Oh, a trigger. Jealousy graced his face and it was pure delight to me. Just what I wanted. An ounce of care on his behalf. Feel the pain and embarrassment I've had to endure these past months we've been together.

"You know, just like Yazzy, Lauryn and all those other hoes are your friends. I can have friends too," I responded to him.

He shook his head, "Naw, not male friends."

"Says who? Rod, you are not my daddy and you can't restrict me."

"Me, if you're gonna be my girl another nigga will not be close to you, point blank." Isn't that the pot calling the kettle black?

"Is that why you blocked my best friend, Aaron from calling my phone?" I didn't wait for a response, I laid it out to him. "I'm not your girl, so I will continue to hang with Xavier, Aaron, and whoever else I chose to."

"No, you won't," he yelled at me.

"Yes, the fuck I will. I don't have time for this." I put what I could into the suitcase, he is not about to turn this shit around on me.

"No, we are not done talking. Are you fucking Xavier?"

"No," I lied, "Is that all you're worried about? If I'm giving this pussy to somebody else. Unlike you, I don't cheat."

"How many times do I have to tell you? I haven't had sex with anybody since we have been together but, you gone fuck around and get Xavier fucked up."

"Rod, don't make those types of threats. I'm not fighting your friends so you will not fight mine."

"I'll show you better than I can tell you," suddenly his phone rung, he answered on the first ring almost like he was anticipating a call, "'Sup," he said into the receiver he looked me up and down. I felt foolish standing there with this heavy ass suitcase waiting for him to finish his phone call. "Either you handle it, or I will," this wasn't a pleasant phone call. "Naw yo' fuck that meet me over there right now I'm about to leave." He ended the call I don't know if it was because I care for him or it was my nosiness, but I wanted to know what was going on. Rod is pissed and only one thing gets him this mad, someone fucking with his money. "We're not done yo' I need you to ride somewhere with me."

"I have somewhere to be." I told Xavier we could hang out tonight.

"No, let's go," he basically dragged me out the front door. We met up with Raymond and Chris. Both brothers looked just as pissed as their brother. I figured it was something drug related. "Stay here yo, I'll be right back," Rod parked and got out the car, he and his brothers stood in the big field in The Bricks before two other guys approached. I wasn't about to watch this boring as drug deal go down, so I called Xavier.

"What's good?" He answered, "I've been texting you."

"I know but I'm with Rod right now."

"Damn, are you serious? Am I gonna be able to see you tonight?"

"I'm not sure, he knows about us going out for coffee apparently one of his friends who works there saw us together. He's not happy about it either."

"What happened to having male friends?"

"Apparently, he does have a problem with it, but I mean you know just as well as I know that we've crossed that friendship line." Just then I noticed Raymond holding Rod back from the two guys they were clearly exchanging heated words my attention was solely on the view.

"Bye, Siah," he said clearly aggravated. "I've been talking, but you're not listening."

"Hold on," I continued to watch Rod try to get to the guys. I could tell it was becoming harder for Raymond to restrain Rod. "If I can't come to see you tonight, I will try tomorrow."

"Iight, I need my dose of you soon though. Hit me up when you can." With Xavier, it's no drama. Just pure fun and great sex. It does help that he knows about Rod and knows we have to be discreet. I enjoy his company.

After hanging up with Xavier, I got out of the car to see exactly what was going on. As soon as I was close enough the conversation was over, and the two guys were walking the other way.

"If they don't have my money by midnight we're popping up. Agreed?"

"Agreed," Raymond and Chris said in unison.

I stood with my arms folded. Just like I thought money was the reason for his anger. When will Rod learn that money isn't everything? "Rod can we go?"

"'Sup Siah? Chris asked I waved at them.

Rod cut his eyes at me. When we got in the car, he started

snapping at me. "This is the type of shit I deal with on a day-to-day basis. Nigga getting product that they either can't sell or end up doing the shit themselves. Motherfuckers take me for a fucking joke Yo. This shit here is enough stress, on top of that I got you coming at me sideways about some bitches that I'm not even fucking with."

"I didn't choose this life for you, you chose it." I gave him the attitude back, "When we met you said you wanted to be a chef, only shit I see you cooking is drug deals. As far as the bitches go, I wouldn't say shit if you didn't do shit." Tears dropped from my eyes like I gave them permission. I can't continue to let this man do this to me there is a high and a low with him no in between. I just want true, untainted love and if I can't get that from Rod then I'll get it from someone else.

He wiped my tears, "Stop crying, yo', I promise, just stick by me and trust me. That petty shit with bitches will never happen again."

"Rod, you make the same promises every time we fall out like this, then you break them. I want to see different I go through shit too, just like you do." I changed the tone of our conversation to something that really matters. "The anniversary of my parents' death is coming up, so I have a lot on my mind. My siblings and I are having a party to celebrate their life, but with all the shit with you I'm not feeling up to it. I want you by my side because I know I might not be able to keep it together, but I don't want any drama or situations with other girls to ruin that day."

"As long as you let me, I will always be by your side. We can overcome all Baby, just believe in me and never leave me."

We left the conversation like that as always, no resolution, no answers just understanding that we love each other and will always be there for each other. He's vague and always have a way of making me forget to confront him about everything I'm hearing around town. I swear he has one more time to let me see him flirt, or even give another bitch attention and the nice girl is out the window. I want to live happily ever after with Rod, but I will not be played for a fool. I'm willing to leave Aaron, Xavier, and Khalil alone if Rod starts acting right and treating me better than he has. I will not be the only one hurt once this relationship is over.

The party turned out better than we all expected. The only family members we invited was Dimanasia. She knows how to party unlike the other ones. Rod came with his crew of men, JP, Lauryn, and his brothers. Emory was stuck to me like glue the entire party trying to avoid Chris. LaKennon sung our parents favorite song which moved almost everyone to tears. The shots that I have been taken all night had me feeling numb. I got emotional earlier, but Rod took me for a walk to talk about my parents. Memories that I will cherish forever. I invited Xavier and his brother, but he hasn't shown up yet. He was in his feelings about Rod and I being back together and me standing him up the other day. I mean I am feeling him, but I can't help where my heart lies. We have been fucking almost every week, but he wants me more than what I can offer him right now. Emory has been seeing Kace as well since she goes with me every time I have a date with Xavier.

After the party Rod and I went back to our apartment. I never officially moved my things out. Well what I thought was going to be at night with just me and him quickly got crushed when Lauryn, Chris and Emory walked in, just like me no matter how hard she tries to stay away from Chris she's drawn right back in.

"Yo Rod we got to go handle some shit." Chris said.

"Like what?" Rod asked with a confused look on his face.

"I got a call from Yazzy, and her she got broken into."

"What they get? And where the fuck was she at? She knows better than to leave my shit unattended."

"It wasn't unattended Lauryn spoke, I took a seat. That's what they ass get, how do you put all that trust into that bitch? "I was there when they came in."

Rod grabbed her throat pulling her scrawny ass closer to him, "what the fuck Lauryn? We've been together all night, and this is the first time you saying shit? How much did they take?" I was scared for her. Not how I wanted to end my night. Emory and I shot each other look. She had informed me about how sketchy Lauryn is and how Khalil don't trust her. Emory said awhile back when Khalil and Rod first started working together Lauryn went behind Rod's back to get product from Khalil, she told him it was for Rod. Long story short, she ended up doing the drugs and Khalil was heated with Rod when money was short. Rod paid the debt, so it was no bad blood between him and Khalil. Rod kicked her ass to the curb, but unfortunately, she apologized and swindled her way back into Rod's life and business. When Emory told me that information, it made sense to why Khalil didn't want her in the room that day I delivered the package for Rod. She's already on thin ice.

"4 pounds," she managed to get out.

"4 fucking pounds?" He said through clenched teeth. "Who was it?"

"I don't know," she fought to say, but Rod was not releasing his grip.

"Rod, yo it ain't her fault." Chris pleaded with his older brother. Rod had a tight grip on Lauryn's throat after a few seconds went by he let her go. She had started to turn another color.

"Who fault is it Chris? I don't see no marks on this bitch indicating she put up a fight for my shit," Rod punched the wall, "I want my shit back tonight and I'm not fucking playing Lauryn." Rod went into our bedroom to calm down and possibly think of a plan to retaliate. We all just sit in silence in disbelief. Who in the world would rob him? Did they not know it was him they were stealing from? I don't know, but I don't want to be involved. Chris and Lauryn started to go out the door.

"Em, you coming?" Chris asked her.

She shook her head, "I can't be in this. My brother won't stand for it."

"Iight, call me later. Hopefully, this isn't your brother's doing."

"What?!" Emory said offended. "My brother is the reason all y'all on, don't ever come out your mouth like that. Stealing from Rod is like Khalil stealing from himself."

"I'm just saying you…"

"Don't say that shit," Emory cut him off, "Besides my brother isn't gonna steal no measly 4 pounds that pennies to him. Lauryn and that bitch knows who did that shit, they probably let the niggas walk right out with it. Probably bagged the shit up for them, then come back with this bogus ass story."

"What? That's crazy as hell. I wouldn't do nothing like that," Lauryn protested.

"I don't trust none of you bitches," Emory spat at her.

"You don't gotta trust me Emory, I don't work for you."

"Bitch not only are you messing with my nigga's money, but you're messing with my brother's money as well, and that shit don't sit right with me. You got off easy tonight because Khalil would do more to you than Rod did, matter of fact let me call my brother now." Emory retrieved her phone from her pocket.

"Yo, it's not that serious to get him involved," Chris protested.

"The fuck it ain't. Hell no, my brother will not be caught up in this shit. Ya'll got niggas stealing from ya'll now, something ain't right."

"Facts, Em," Rod said in agreement with Emory. "All this shit needs to be handled now. Somebody is fucking with me and I will find out who it is." Rob grabbed my hand leading into the bedroom. "Yo, I need you to lay low tonight I don't know what's going to happen so stay at your sisters' crib."

"I don't know Rod, this shit sounds very dangerous and I have a bad feeling about this."

"I got this Babe. I'll see you later." He kissed me before walking out the room, as much as I don't like the situation, I guess I have to support my man even though it makes me so anxious. We've been back together for five minutes then all this shit happens. When I came from the room, I was surprised to still see Emory and Lauryn sitting on my couch.

"Why the fuck is she still here?" I asked Emory.

"We're babysitting," Emory laughed rolling her eyes.

"I'm going to find Rod, so we know who stole from him." I said boldly, if I'm going to be a part of Rod's life, I need to do this. I'm not going to be sitting around worrying if he's going to be alright. I'm gonna be right there front and center. Fucking with him is like fucking with me.

"Let's go...what about her?" Emory said.

"She can come, but if we find out she's the one being disloyal, I'm gonna beat her ass myself." Enough of the quiet girl I'm all in now and I'm ready for whatever and it helps that Emory is too.

CHAPTER 15

After driving around town to Rod's normal spots we finally got word that he was in The Bricks, we met up with him Chris and Raymond. Yazzy was standing with them. He tried to protest us coming, but ultimately, he gave me their whereabouts. They stood in the parking lot of the most hung out spot in The Bricks. Of course, it was packed with a lot of people like it was the club. The three of us walked up to them.

"So, what's up," Emory asked the brothers. She'd called Khalil on the way over to give him a heads up to check his stash houses just in case this wasn't an isolated incident. Hearing his voice on her speaker made my heart drop. Although the head was trash, it can't get out.

"Word on the street, this nigga Jay out here getting right," Chris answered he pulled Emory in awfully close to him. Guess to make Yazzy feel some type of way.

"So?" I wanted to know.

"We're waiting, I called that nigga." Rod said.

Minutes later a group of five guys came up to where we were. "What's goodie, Rod?" The leader of the pack said I assumed he's Jay.

"You tell me," Rod dapped him. "Word is you ran in Yazzy's shit and stole some bags." Rod was calm, cool, and collected.

"Word from who?"

"My nigga, did you do it or not?" The crowd began to surround us, most of them with their phones out recording. News Bern.

Jay turned to his crew then back at Rod with the smirk. Rod punched him in the mouth. When his crew tried to buck up to help him, Chris and Raymond pulled out their guns and cocked them, pointing at them daring them to take another step. Rod was pounding into Jay, kicking him in the face. "Where is my shit at nigga?" He asked in between blows but Jay said nothing. Rod kept on beating, full of rage. It was hard to sit there watching something like this go down, but I guess in these streets if you go for anything more people will try to try you.

"Rod, maybe it wasn't him," Yazzy called out.

"Who the fuck was it then?" I answered for him I had a feeling this hoe knew more than she was letting on.

She shrugged her shoulders, "I don't know, I wasn't there." Now everybody turned to Lauryn. Rod stopped putting the beating on Jay.

"That bitch let me in, she owes me. I didn't know it was your shit Rod I swear," Jay had blood dripping from his mouth as he pointed to Lauryn.

Rod wiped the blood from Jay on his white shirt. The bitch didn't have anything to say for herself. I just knew something was fishy with her story. Chris and Raymond put their guns away as Jay's crew helped him to his feet. I watched Rod, and his face went from angry to disappointed. I think he was more disappointed with himself for trusting his so-called best friend again. Rod stepped to me, "Beat her ass," he whispered in my ear. Without hesitation I pounced on Lauryn. I planted blows all over her face. I could hear Emory cheering me on. I sat on her chest, with one hand I pounded into her face with the other I held onto her hair she tried to fight back, but I didn't let up on my assault. Rob pulled me off for her. As I stood over her, I spit in her face. That'll teach her lame ass to not fuck with Rod no more, because she knew Jay was after her and brought that heat around. As I looked at Lauryn on the ground, I'm impressed with the beat I just gave her. Being that this is my first fight and all, but Rod fueled me with all the gas I needed.

"You're wild yo,", Rod laughed. He dismissed Jay and his crew, he did apologize to Jay for how everything went down, but made it noticeably clear to him that he wanted his product back and that Lauryn was his problem now.

Yazzy helped Lauryn up. Her face was beginning to swell,

"I'm sorry Rod," she said to him. She stared at him hoping for his forgiveness.

"Bitch don't say shit else to me. Do you know how ugly shit would've gotten with Jay?" He paused, "Yeah you know. I'm done with both of you."

"Me? Wait, Rod I didn't do shit," Yazzy pleaded to him

"I don't know Yazzy you're fucking with Lauryn the long way and I can't trust it."

"Fuck her if that stops our business." She let Lauryn fall back to the ground.

"No, I'm out. Your shit is getting swept as we speak."

"How am I going to pay my rent?"

"That's not my problem." Police sirens filled the quiet night, "We're out."

Back at the apartment Rod immediately got in the shower, my knuckles were bruised from the fight. As I rubbed my knuckles my mind kept drifting off to Rod paying Yazzy's rent. I should have known because this bitch doesn't have a job. How long has he been taking care of her? It doesn't matter that he was paying it so he could trap out her house. I'm going to keep my mouth shut about it since now it's all over. He got word that Jay returned what he had taken from Yazzy's apartment. The fate of Lauryn is up to Jay, but I have a feeling it's not going to be good. This is the second time she has put Rod in a bind and hopefully it's the last. She's no best friend doing the things she does to jeopardize his reputation and business.

"Thanks Baby," Rod said holding me tight. "You were really there for me tonight."

"And thank you because you were there for me tonight as well," I said referring to the party for my parents. The party seemed like a distance memory against all that had occurred afterwards.

"Can we be together again? For real?"

"We can definitely work on it," Being with Rod today made me realize that he's the one for me. No matter how much I try to fight it he's the one.

CHAPTER 16

After that night with Jay and Lauryn drama we've been good. No bitches, no coming home late, or arguments. Rod and I made special plans for us to spend all day together and try to rekindle everything that we have lost in the last few months. We've been going on dates regularly. I haven't seen this side of him in a long time and I love it. I opted out telling him about Xavier, Khalil, and Aaron because it will only do harm to our relationship. I got up to shower and to cook breakfast I'm so happy in this relationship right now. After breakfast we went shopping in Jacksonville. He brought me everything I wanted. I've been telling him that I want to dabble in photography, and he's got me a camera, tripod, and a software to edit my photos. I'm so grateful for him and since he supported me in my dreams, I got him a chef knife set, apron, pots and pans and a cookbook. I look forward to watching him whip up delicious meals in our kitchen.

I don't really know about this whole Teana chick, and where she stands in his life. But I vow to find out very soon. "Who is that?" I asked Rod, who was texting somebody.

"Just Q, he keeps fucking shit up," we put the bags into the trunk before getting into the car.

"What's wrong?" Over this past year I learned many things about Q. For starters, this whole drug operation started with him. He was on fire in the beginning, but he started getting products from plugs and could sell it. He looped in his brothers, but when Q got arrested for selling to an undercover the responsibility ended up being given to Rod. He put his all into it. He expanded to cross country plugs moving more weight than anyone in New Bern. He put them on the right track by taking risks everyone else is afraid to take. Lately, Rod has been telling me that Q has been asking for more work but he's always messing something up. One day he took the wrong product to a potential big-time client. Rod had to swoop in to save the day, as usual. Q has been off his game, but Rod is being secretive as to the reason why. My mind wanders and the only excuse I can think of is that he's using, hardcore.

"Nothing, when we get back to New Bern before we go to dinner, I need to go handle this drop and Q."

Well there goes our day. Luckily, I have something to take care of. Xavier has been blowing me up all day long. Rod dropped me off to our apartment, I got into my car and headed to Xavier's house. I pounded on the door.

"Damn, you can't answer my calls or texts, but you can pop up?" Xavier said when he opened the door. He tried to hide his smile, but I know he's happy to see me. Truth be told, I'm happy to see him too. Life with Rod is going great, but why do I keep thinking about Xavier. It doesn't help that regardless of how many times I ignore his phone calls or messages he's still happy to have any time with me.

"I can leave," I acted like I was going to walk away.

He grabbed my wrist, "Hell no, get your ass in here." I followed him into his bedroom. We quickly undressed and had sex on his bedroom floor. "Please tell me you can get away later," Xavier said while I got dressed.

"I don't know," In fact, I did know. There is no way I was getting away from Rod tonight. This meeting was by chance.

"Just tell him I'm painting you or something."

I laughed, "He's not going to go for that. I have to go, I will text you later. And you do owe me a painting."

"Iight," he gripped my ass as we shared a kiss.

This shit is getting stressful. I have Xavier craving all my attention, Aaron wanting either me to come back for a visit or him to come here. Khalil's been asking for another taste. Then Rod gets all my love and attention. Rod is very sexually active, and we've been having sex multiples times a day. My poor vagina is tired, she's incredibly pleased, but tired.

Rod and I have dinner plans at this new restaurant downtown New Bern. He still wasn't back at the apartment by the time I finished with Xavier. To keep my reservation, I sat there awaiting his arrival. I texted him letting him know to meet me at the restaurant. I ordered a pina colada for my wait and browsed through social media. Rod said twenty minutes, but it's been well over thirty minutes. I'm getting more and more irritated with the waiter, so I ordered another pina colada.

"This one is on me," Xavier sat my drink down in front of me. I almost shitted my pants. Rod could be here any minute. Is Xavier following me?

"Thank you," I tried to hide the shocked and terrified look on my face. "What are you doing here?"

"Working, I didn't know you were coming here. We could have ridden together."

"Yeah, no. I'm meeting Rod."

"Oh, that's why you rushed out." I nodded my head.

"Sorry Baby," Rod came from behind us, he bent down to kiss me. "I had to make one last stop." He said across from me. My heart dropped. I prayed silently for Xavier to walk away so Rod and I can enjoy our dinner. "Oh shit, what's good X, are you our waiter?" I sipped my drink. Rod is trying to be funny, he knows this man is not our waiter.

"Naw man, I'm just speaking to an old friend."

"Iight cool, time to go then," Rod stared at Xavier.

"Rod!" I shot him a look because he is being rude. He also shot me with a look that entailed I had one second to get away from this table before it got ugly. "I'll see you later Xavier," I said to him.

"No, you won't," Rod snapped, and Xavier walked away defeated and I feel bad. Rod's jealousy turned me on though. "What are you getting?" he asked.

"First, a shot of rum," I flagged down a nearby server to let her know that I wanted another drink. She informed me that she was going to send our server to our table momentarily. "I want a bloody steak."

"Blood?" he asked in disgust. I nodded I love a bloody ass pink, juicy steak. That's the way my daddy used to eat it. "Imma stick with a burger."

Moments later our waitress came to our table to take our order. I read her name tag, Tateana. Just the bitch I wanted to see. I had Emory do an investigation and this is the only night she works. I intentionally and quickly made reservations for this. There she was standing there with a bulging belly, very much pregnant. When she noticed who was at the table her mouth dropped. She glared at Rod, but he seemed unbothered.

"Can I get you guys started off with any appetizers? I recommend the spinach dip." She nervously said.

"I recommend the fucking truth," I sipped on my pina colada and glared at her.

CHAPTER 17

I want answers and if I can't get those answers from Rod, then why not his supposedly baby mama Teana. Before Rod and I can fully move on the slate has to be cleared. I must know that my heart is protected. They both tried to play it cool, but I know something is going on between them. There's no way that he can get out of this one.

I clarified my response to her, "I'll pass on the appetizers for right now, my only question to you is what is going on between you and my man?"

She looked at me and then back at Rod, "This is very unprofessional and tacky to come to my job to address this." She looked around the restaurant, making sure none of her co-workers were nearby.

"Bitch, I don't give a fuck about your job. We can do this the easy way or the hard way. But either way, it's going to get done," I snapped at her.

"Nothing is *going on* between me and Rod. I'm pregnant but it is not Rod's."

"Which time? Because months back you were claiming you were pregnant by Rod so I'm very confused." Rod sat there letting me hash everything out with this Teana. This time jealousy was written all over me.

"When you and Rod first got together, I admit I was a bit jealous, because me and him were talking prior. I've always been Rod's girl so to have you come along and jeopardize my future with him, I was upset so I lied. Rod knows that he's not the father of my child and not that it matters but Quinton is my child's father."

I don't know how much of the story from this Teana I can believe. I looked over at Rod, "Is this true?" I asked him and he nodded his head, then it all started to make sense back at the Thanksgiving dinner Q and Rod were fussing about Teana, but what I still don't get is why did he leave my house that night to go over her house. This shit is so fucking weird and I'm over it. But I want answers and I want them sooner than later, so I asked, "That night when me and Em showed up at your doorstep, what was that shit about?"

"That was me trying to get back with Rod, but Q had already told him about us hooking up. I don't want Q, I want Rod." She said boldly.

"Well the difference between Q and Rod is that Rod is taken, and this girl isn't going anywhere. When was the last time you and Rod were together? Because before you said ya'll were still sleeping together, I'm just trying to understand your lies."

"It's been a while."

I looked at her sideways, "how long is a while?"

"Not since you came in town," she pouted.

"Why lie?"

"Because I was still in love with him, and Rod flirts so much. I never knew when it was for real. He never been with anyone serious, other than me. It seemed serious with ya'll and I didn't like that."

"That's some homewrecker shit," she is annoying and childish. How could he fall for a bitch like this?

"Well lucky for you, Rod is a keeper and I wish I hadn't fucked it up. He's faithful. Rod likes to act like he does a lot of shit but when he's with a girl seriously he's with only her. When we were together, I did get jealous of the number of girls that was getting his attention, but he never strayed ever. What about you?"

"What?" I like her nerve. She doesn't know the Rod I know. He never strayed with her, but he has admitted to letting females give him head earlier on in our relationship, and that is a form of cheating. I doubt if that was new behavior. Maybe she was just too dumb to find out what he was doing when he was out in the streets.

"You heard me, you don't know Rod like I know Rod. So, it's

only natural that when he's around females you think he's fucking them, but contrary to your belief Honey, Rod hasn't fucked anyone but you. Rod may be a lot of things but he's loyal that much I know so there's no doubt in my mind that he's being loyal to you. I wish that weren't the case because I will love to have one more time with him. But chicks like you take him for granted." Has he been talking to her about me? He can't fault me for thinking the worse.

Rod was soaking up all the compliments that she was giving him, but are they true? Have I been thinking this whole time we've been together that he's been playing me when he's not? I actually started to feel guilty, what a way to make a fool out of myself, nobody was playing me I've been playing my damn self. "Rod?" He looked over at me.

Teana said, "If that's all you want to know from me, I'll give you some time to look over the menu." She went on her way.

"What's up?" I said to Rod, "why didn't you ever tell me?"

"I was hoping you would learn to trust me. This street shit is a persona and I told you that a long time ago. But you let shit get to you then you decided to doubt me."

"I wouldn't have doubted you if you had just told me."

"I did numerous of times. One, I told you I would never cheat on you after I told you about bitches giving me dome. I told you that flirting comes with the job I have. I'm not like these other dudes out here anymore and sometimes they say I'm soft. I had a long talk with my mom, and she told me to stop playing with your heart, and I have. My main focus is you, nobody else. I want *you* forever Baby."

The way Rod was talking to me right now made me feel all bubbly inside I let my mind and my insecurities get the best of me. It made me doubt him and not trust him. I got into my own head, and now I've fucked everything up. I have to come clean about my infidelities. I can't allow my wrongs to hang over us for the rest of our lives. Even though the secrets will never get out, I will not be able to live with myself knowing I'm lying to him every day. I sat in silence during the remainder of dinner. Talk about speechless. To move forward, the truth has to come out. "Rod, we have to talk." I said to him once we got back home. I took my shoes off at the door then sat on the couch. He joined me and I went for it, "I love you so much, but what I'm going to say will hurt our relationship."

He stared at me, "Are you fucking somebody else?"

I paused before answering, "Yes."

"What the fuck, Si?" Rod put his hands over his face, "Who?"

"I don't think that matters."

Rod raised his voice, "Who are you fucking with? Huh?" I didn't say anything. I'm so scared of what he will do. "Answer me baby please," Rod said softly.

"I slept with Aaron, Xavier, and fooled around with Khalil," I said plainly as my heart thumped.

Rod jumped up from the couch, "How could you do me like this?" He started to cry. "What the fuck yo? Three niggas? Am I not good enough for you?" Tears streamed from his beautiful face. Tears I put there.

"Baby, you are good enough. I fucked up and I'm sorry," I reached out to him, but he pulled away from me.

"Get out my fucking house," Rod said through clenched teeth.

"Rod!"

"Fuck you, you're passing pussy out to all these niggas. I don't want you anymore. I'm not sharing with no one. You were supposed to be mine, only mine." Rod started to cry harder.

"Rod, I'm sorry. I promise I will end it all."

"You got to go Yo, we are done."

"No, I don't want to be without you," my own tears started to fall, but Rod wasn't interested. He didn't want me anywhere near him.

"Get out! I'll get movers to bring your things to your sister's house."

"Please, let's talk this out."

"It's done. You have community pussy now. You're not different from these New Bern hoes. Now go," Rod grabbed me and pushed me out the front door. He closed the door in my face, tossing my shoes, phone, and keys out with me. I banged on the door to no avail. I sobbed by the door repeating multiple times how sorry I am. Two hours went by and I was still at the door trying to get Rod to open it. I finally picked myself up and went to my siblings' house. I locked the bedroom door behind me, wrapped myself in the covers and cried. Just like that, in the blink of an eye our relationship is ruined and over. I've done to Rod what countless of other girls have done to him, cheat and lie. He's been protecting his heart the entire time, but I still broke it. I have broken us.

The very next morning after the worst night of my life I received a text from Rod saying, 'check on your boy', my eyes were so swollen I could barely make out the words. I texted Xavier but no answer. I called him, still no answer. This cannot be good. My mind began to race, what has Rod done? I started to panic because I never want anyone to get hurt. After about 30 calls to Xavier back-to-back, I finally got an answer, but Xavier was not on the other end of the phone call it was Kace. "Hello," I said into the receiver.

"Right now is not the best time, Siah."

"Where is Xavier?"

"Siah, I will call you back we are at the hospital right now."

My heart dropped, "What happened?" I said a silent prayer for the unknown.

"I can't talk right now, but I promise I will call you back." Kace said before disconnecting the call. I want answers right now I thought to myself, but I guess I will have to wait. Rod has given me the impression that he does something to Xavier, but what? After last night I thought he was done with me, so why do something to Xavier? I dialed Rod's number, surprisingly he answered on the first ring.

"What's up?" he asked nonchalantly.

"Rod, don't play what is going on?"

"Did you not call to check on your boy?"

"I did, but he couldn't answer. What did you do?"

"You call to check on that nigga before calling me? That's another reason why I'm done with your bitch ass. Just know that every time I see that nigga, I'll fucking him up. And let your little friend step foot in North Carolina, and I'm fucking him up too."

"What's the point if we're done? I understand you don't want to be with me. I will leave you alone, and in return just leave me alone to deal with it all."

"No, Bitch, I'm never leaving you the fuck alone, you're going to pay for the shit that you've done to me. Better yet you might want to call the auto shop for some new tires." *Call disconnected.*

I rushed to the window to look at my car, all my tires were slashed. I rushed outside to evaluate the damage to my car. I began to sob. Rod is taking this shit too fucking far. I called him back, "Why are you doing this? You can't fuck with my personal items. My parents brought me that car." I cried harder remembering the day my parents surprised Shae and I with the matching cars. "If you were honest with me, I wouldn't have fucked other people."

"No, you fucked who you fucked because you a hoe ass bitch. You are a nasty ass hoe and I am going to expose you for the whore that you are."

"I know you're hurt and believe me I am too. But I have agreed to give you space now it's time for you to give me mine. I know I fucked up, but all of this is uncalled for. It's stupid and childish. You can go back to fucking with the hoes that want you so bad and let me be."

"Seems like the only hoe I had was you. Shit don't work like that Si. I can't let this shit go. It's fucked up." He took a moment to catch his breath. I could hear the pain in his voice. "Did you fuck them like you fucked me?"

"I'm not having this conversation with you. Just know that I love you."

He laughed, "Answer my question. Did you suck their dicks like you sucked mine?"

"This is rude and disrespectful, and I refuse to have this conversation with you." The nature of the sex I had with either one of them is irrelevant. His own insecurities started to settle in.

"That's cool," he said.

"Did you do something bad to Xavier?" I questioned.

He sighed heavily, "I confronted him about you. We fought."

"You put him in the hospital?"

"I had a lot on my mind. That bitch ass nigga will survive though. I'll send him some flowers," he laughed.

"Rod?" Now that he was calm, we can have a serious conversation.

"Yes, I'll send a tow truck for your car. I'll pay for the tires Yo, and I'll stop fucking with you. You have to understand, every girl I've ever been with has cheated on me. I'm not the best boyfriend, but I work hard to live the life I live. I wanted to be different with you, for you. I failed."

"I'm so sorry. I love you so much." I wish we were different, I wish our relationship were different. We have changed so much. We grew separately, he'd has already experienced so much in life where I have not. As crazy as it sounds, I needed to explore to make sure he was the one for me. He'd already explored and knew I was the one for him. Thinking back to the first time we met made me smile. "Do you still think we can overcome anything?"

He sighed but didn't answer immediately. Minutes passed as he thought about how to respond. "Not right now, I need time." *Call disconnected.*

I have to respect his answer. I went back inside the house after the tow truck came to get my car. Kace called me back letting me know Xavier had a concussion from the fight with Rod, but he was going to be fine. Xavier didn't want to talk to me, and I completely understand. I flipped through the pictures of Rod and I on my phone all night long and cried myself to sleep.

CHAPTER 18

I live for love, I'm alive because of love, I have nothing in me but to love and I now know that when I love, I love hard. I'm so confused right now with my life and I'm not sure where I go from here all I know is that I'm going to love and respect myself way more than I expect a man to. Temporary emotions are just that… temporary. What my parents had was long lasting, am I wrong for wanting the same thing? Nevertheless, I will take time to focus more on myself then maybe Rod will forgive me, and we can be together.

I cut all ties with Xavier and Khalil. To add more fuel to my fucked-up life, I told Emory about me and Khalil. She was beyond pissed and haven't talked to me since. She says that was the main reason she did not want to introduce me to her family. She'll get over it. Cutting ties with Aaron was more difficult because we have known each other for so long. Olivia left him once he told her about our affair. He and I are taking a break from each other right now. We will always be friends, but we cannot and will not have sex anymore. My siblings and I are living wonderfully under the same roof. Raymond and Shae are doing great, Peanut and Kendra are back together, and Kennon found him a little girlfriend. Everyone is happy, but me. I hurt Rod so bad and now I will live with him never forgiving me. I never loved anyone else, but him. Hopefully one day he will love me again. I'm waiting for that day. In the meantime, I'm getting myself together, I started doing photography full time. Taking pictures of family, friends, and historic downtown New Bern.

CPSIA information can be obtained
at www.ICGtesting.com
Printed in the USA
BVHW031054260620
582396BV00004B/20/J

9 781984 584793